"Steeped in Celtic mythology and music, and accurate Irish history, particularly of the Great Hunger, spiced with glimpses of the supernatural, *Looking for Cornelius* by Diana Hayes is a satisfying story, set mostly in Ireland, of a young woman's search for her Irish great-grandfather while accompanying her thirteen-year-old fiddle student to compete for a music scholarship in Cork City. The writing is tight and often poetic, the research and descriptions of Irish locations are impeccable, and the plot twists are not foreseeable and so most pleasing. A must—and not only for lovers of Irish stories."

—PATRICK TAYLOR
Author of *An Irish Country Doctor*

"In *Looking for Cornelius*, Diana Hayes takes readers through an Irish landscape haunted by stone circles and ancient monastic ruins, lingering at lakes where saints performed miracles. We accompany Deirdre, a music teacher from Montreal, and her student Éamon, a gifted young fiddler, to Cork so that Éamon can audition for a place in a prestigious music program. Both are also searching for answers to the old riddles of family and belonging. Threaded through the narrative phrases of poetry and of folk songs in Gaeilge and English serve as both gorgeous soundtrack and field guide to this rich and lyrical novella. The novella is a special form, providing a meeting place for the intersection of characters and elliptical storytelling; *Looking for Cornelius* occupies this space beautifully and memorably."

—THERESA KISHKAN
Author of *The Weight of the Heart*

Looking for Cornelius

Looking for Cornelius

A Novella

DIANA HAYES

RESOURCE *Publications* · Eugene, Oregon

LOOKING FOR CORNELIUS
A Novella

Resource Publications
An Imprint of Wipf and Stock Publishers
199 W. 8th Ave., Suite 3
Eugene, OR 97401

www.wipfandstock.com

PAPERBACK ISBN: 979-8-3852-5033-2
HARDCOVER ISBN: 979-8-3852-5034-9
EBOOK ISBN: 979-8-3852-5035-6

VERSION NUMBER 06/27/25

for my sisters,
Maureen Mary and Patricia Lynn

and for Alana Doyle

Contents

Contents

Permissions

Extract from lyrics of "The Fields of Athenry" by Pete St. John, used by permission of the Pete St. John Estate. Dublin, Ireland.

Extract from "The Well of Grief" from *River Flow: New and Selected Poems* by David Whyte, used by permission of Many Rivers Company, Langley, WA. www.davidwhyte.com.

Extract from "St. Kevin and the Blackbird" from *Field Work* by Seamus Heaney, used by permission of Faber and Faber Ltd., Essex UK.

Acknowledgments

Many thanks to:

My husband, Peter Southam, first reader of the manuscript, for his love and patience. I couldn't have managed the intensity of writing this story without his calming and supportive influence.

My father, John Louis Hayes, who started me on the Irish family research path many years ago. Bless his soul, now in *Annwn,* the Otherworld, likely having a pint of Guinness with old Cornelius.

My sisters, Maureen and Lynn, who have always encouraged me in my genealogy research. I have vivid memories of my journey to Ireland with Lynn when we took a similar route as Deirdre and Éamon, visiting many of the places that are highlighted in this novella.

Alana Doyle, who visited Salt Spring Island in 2016 to give a writing workshop which sparked the nucleus for this novella. Many thanks for her careful review of the manuscript-in-progress and her helpful, intuitive editing and feedback.

Lorraine Gane, who mentored me through the early stages of writing my novella and provided timely feedback and encouragement.

Theresa Kishkan, who read the manuscript in an early form and provided valuable suggestions.

Patrick Taylor, who provided expert feedback and encouraging words.

Alane Lalonde, always there for me, who provided moral support and shares the same love and curiosity about ancestry and family history.

My cousins Lynda Incobourg and Robert Maunder, who provided important details about Cornelius Alfred and William James. We share direct family ties to Great-Grandfather Cornelius—Cornelius Eoin Ó hAodha of Skibbereen, as he is known in my novella.

Freddie White, a masterful guitar player, singer-songwriter, and interpreter of songs from Cobh, County Cork, for granting permission to appear as Éamon's hero and perform at Kelly's Bar in Cobh in my novella.

Terri Kearney and Philip O'Regan of Cunnamore, County Cork, for making their book *Skibbereen: The Famine Story* and their DVD *The Great Irish Famine, Remembering Skibbereen* available and doing such important work at the Skibbereen Heritage Centre to educate visitors about *An Gorta Mór*.

Jerry Mulvihill, author of *The Truth Behind the Irish Famine, 1845–52*. His book is an important and comprehensive account of *An Gorta Mór*, which includes seventy-two paintings that were commissioned for the book.

Hannah Harris, Irish fiddler and singer, who provided valuable information about traditional Irish music.

The editors of *The Galway Review*, who published an earlier version of my novella chapter titled "The Graves are Walking," spring 2025 edition.

My editor at Wipf and Stock, Matt Wimer, who gave my novella the perfect home and guided me through each step of the process.

List of Illustrations

Map of Ireland provided by Pat Walker, Illustrator

Map of County Cork provided by Peter P. Southam

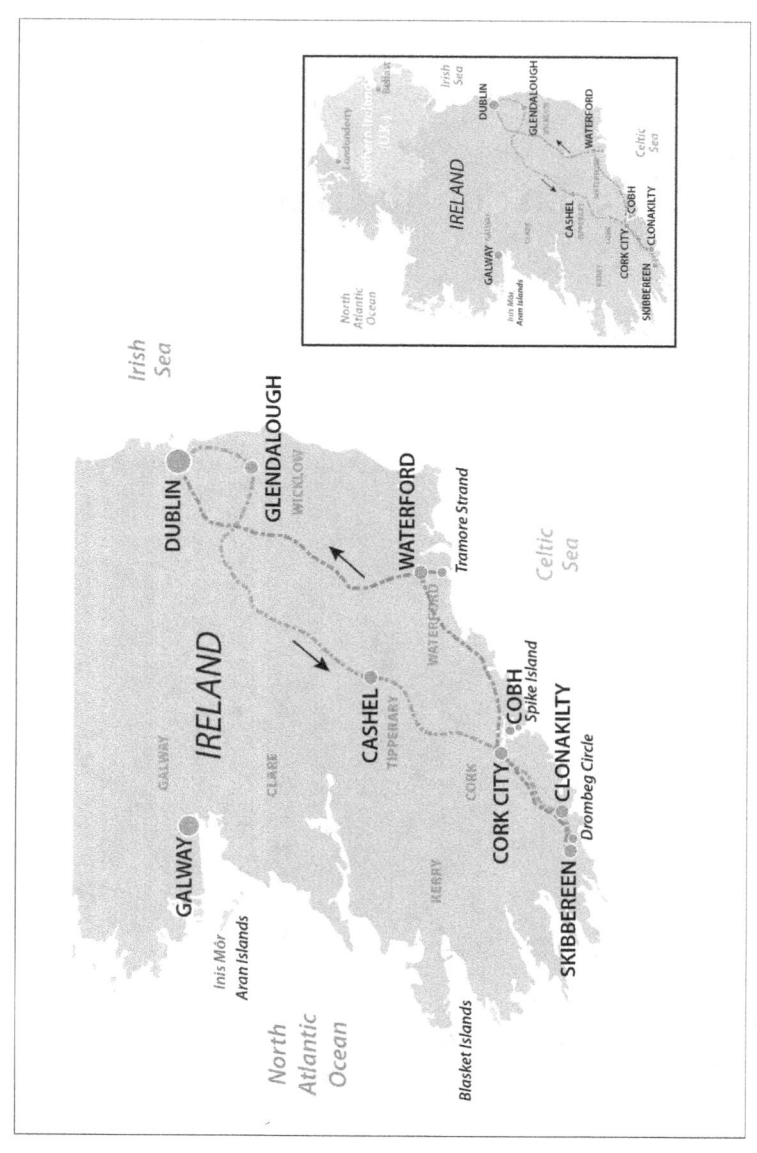

Irish Sea

DUBLIN

GLENDALOUGH

WICKLOW

WATERFORD

Tramore Strand

WATERFORD

Celtic Sea

CASHEL

TIPPERARY

COBH

Spike Island

CORK CITY

CORK

CLONAKILTY

SKIBBEREEN

Drombeg Circle

IRELAND

GALWAY

GALWAY

CLARE

KERRY

Inis Mór
Aran Islands

Blasket Islands

North
Atlantic
Ocean

Irish
Sea

IRELAND

North
Atlantic
Ocean

Inis Mór
Aran Islands

Londonderry

Northern Ireland
(U.K.)

Dublin

DUBLIN

GLENDALOUGH

WATERFORD

Celtic
Sea

GALWAY

CASHEL

COBH

CORK CITY

CLONAKILTY

SKIBBEREEN

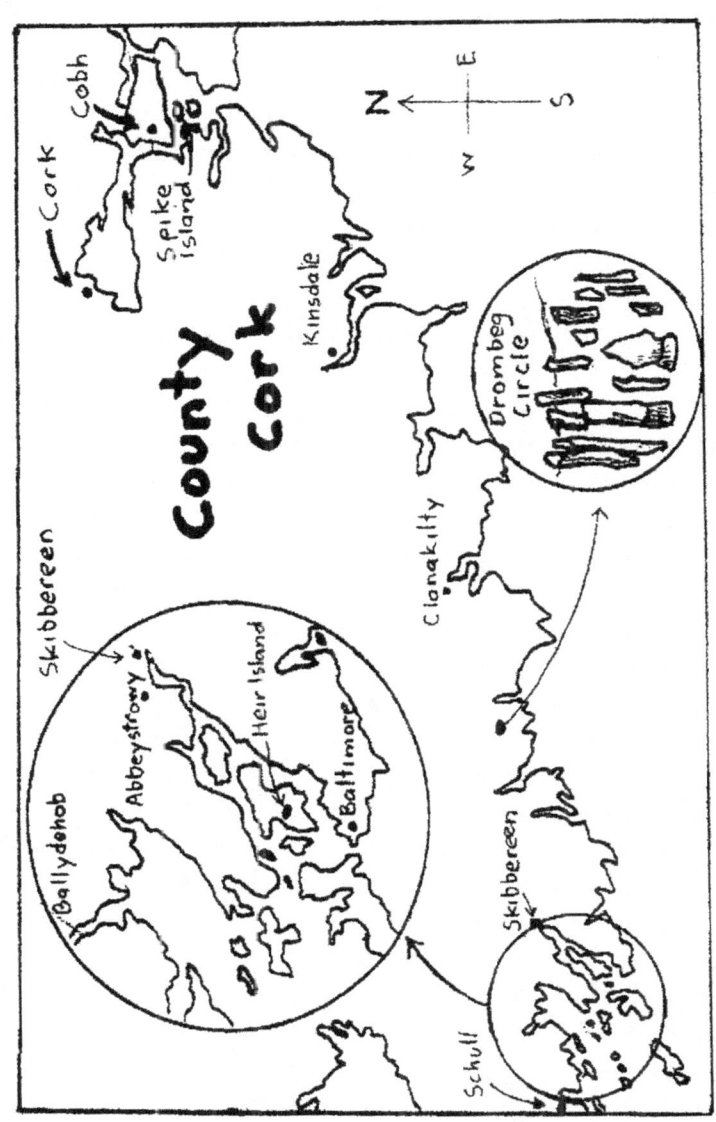

County Cork

Cork
Cobh
Spike Island
Kinsdale
Drombeg Circle
Clonakilty
Skibbereen
Skibbereen
Ballydehob
Abbeystrowry
Heir Island
Baltimore
Schull

N E S W

PART ONE

Fiddles and Fire

Ó hAodha, Family Clan of County Cork
Descendants of fire—the cauldron's flame
Famine ships named after the girls
Holy Hannah, Bright Maeve
Priestess of Skibbereen
This cartography of genes[1]

—DIANA HAYES, FROM "NOTATIONS ON A MAP"

The Ogham Pendant
—I Am an Orphan Girl

DEIRDRE WOKE WITH A startle, her mauve cotton nightshirt drenched from sweat, her curly hair even curlier with warmth rising like a prescient mist. *Descendants of fire,* she dreamed—her family clan emerging from the cauldron's flame.

"Oh, it must be old Cornelius again, knocking on the door," she mumbled to no one in particular. The sun wasn't even up yet.

According to the late-night meandering stories shared by her papa, Great-Grandfather Cornelius Ó hAodha had always been a mischief-maker and had the gift of second sight. With a wily smile and a gleam in those handsome hazel eyes, Cornelius would recite a poetic couplet or two and then throw in lines from an Irish rebel song, maybe "The Sea Around Us," or "Rising of the Moon." He was a *Chucky* at heart, *Tiocfaidh ár lá*—our day will come. Out of the foggy dreamscape on nights when Deirdre was most troubled, he would hand her an oar and a whiskey, nudging her to take notice, row toward the synchronicities, listen for the messages in song. *Tune your antennae,* he might have whispered. *The old country is communicating with you.* Yes, this she trusted implicitly.

Well, I might as well just rise and begin my day, she thought. Make her favorite espresso and potato pancakes which she cooked in batches for the week, complete with Kate Kearney's marmalade, her absolute favorite. It was not yet dawn but she had plenty to do before classes began at nine o'clock.

Deirdre had been a teacher of traditional Irish music at the Academy of St. Anne's in Montreal for five years. Her pupils were disadvantaged inner-city children with the talent of angels but no opportunity to explore their gifts until a grant from city council had answered Deirdre's prayers and made her dream job possible. She had played fiddle in an Irish traveling band in clubs for nearly eight years, scraping by and honing her own quirky style of music and song while working a variety of day jobs along the way, house-keeping being the most lucrative.

The children were her trusted charges and those chosen for the Trifinity program were exceptional, passionate about the old Irish lyrics and compositions especially after she told them about the stories within the stories. Their blood was at least as thick as hers with Munster genes even if the lineage dated back several cen-turies. One boy in her class, not yet thirteen, still had that awkward voice change that cracked and broke into the silence of her class-room. He was onto something only his family could recognize. Éamon was different, an indigo child as they call them now—rare gifts with unruly intelligence. He would disappear into the music as an oarsman slips off the edge of the world, beyond the veil to a place only his imagination could follow, beyond the rogue waves of a mid-Atlantic Sea. A prodigy of the fiddle, he played flawlessly by ear after hearing the music only once.

Deirdre showered and put on her turquoise skirt and maroon jumper, a pair of well-worn Aussie Blundstones, then dragged a brush through her tightly wound curls. Copper-colored, she was always teased for that head of tangles along with her one-of-a-kind style in her class. All hair and no patience, the teachers would complain. Eyes greener than hazel, with flecks of amber, her hands were instruments of her heritage, long delicate fingers articulat-ing the secret cipher of the Gammon. The fiddle bow fit naturally between thumb and fingers, like an extension of her graceful arms and wrists. The fiddle she had picked out at a secondhand mu-sic shop was her treasure. It was made from scratch specifically for left-handed players. The bow moved like a feather persuad-ing the air, inviting complex sounds, soulful ballads, with lyrics by O'Reiley or maybe Finnagan, and on Sundays, a prayer for St. Brigid of Kildare, mother saint of Ireland.

Deirdre had a small statue of St. Brigid holding the sacred flame. She knew the Celtic goddess worked miracles, including healing and feeding the poor. Brigid's Church of the Oak was situated on the site of the pagan shrine to the fifth-century goddess, served by a group of seven women who tended the eternal flame. Her small oratory included a school of art for metalwork and illuminations. Her scriptorium produced the illumined Book of Kildare (alas, lost forever) with the assistance of the hermit monk, Conleth. Brigid's relics are now safely sleeping in the tomb of her brothers Patrick and Columba. Her feast day fell on Imbolc, February 1st, marking the closing of winter storms and the possibilities of spring in the old country.

Deirdre walked over to the clothes bureau, not bothered by the creaking boards on her third-floor brownstone walk-up. It was a small apartment that she had decorated with colors and textiles, painting surfaces that needed her attention and detailing the old oak floors so that they shone like earlier incarnations of the room. Floors were her specialty when it came to setting up a home away. At every fork in her path, humble apartments had grown to be sanctuaries, nests of safety, where she placed the collection of stones and shells from her travels, hoping their luck would see her through to brighter times.

She reached into her music box for the pendant and chain she reserved for special concerts and found her hand was empty. Where could she have left it? How many times had it reappeared over the years in a window ledge or next to her bed? Once she had left it on the bedside table of a short-lived lover who held it in trust a little too long, leaving her with great anxiety and regret. It was as though he knew just how important the necklace was to her, and how it conjured voices of her past. With a sigh of relief and shame, she collected it days later from his mail slot where he had grudgingly placed it for her to retrieve.

"Everything in its rightful place," she mumbled, sighing as she turned on the bureau lamp to take a closer look. Gone. Pendant and chain not to be seen. She must have left it next to the kitchen sink last evening when she came home tired and hungry, rushing through her wind-down routine to put a small plate of cheese and biscuits on the table. Too late in the evening for a proper supper, Deirdre was a master of impromptu teatimes. Snacks were her specialty. The washing up was just as important as her delight in simple food as she took the extra time to enjoy late-night radio and her favorite music programs while scrubbing the pots.

She checked the kitchen and the hallway table for her Ogham pendant. This was no ordinary necklace. She had seen it in a secondhand shop called Tinkers on Eglington when she was window-shopping with Grannie Moll in Toronto's Yorkville district. Moll bought it for her as an early birthday present. She knew the Ogham now by instinct and could spot it miles away. Deirdre had studied the stone monuments in the west of Ireland in a book by Damian McManus. She knew the stories intimately as though her own hands had hewn the surfaces, carrying out the message from her far-away ancestors. Ogham, named after *Oghma*, the Celtic god of elocution or fine speech, was the first written language of Ireland which was used primarily for territorial or mortuary stones. This was understood by those who attended the wakes. They knew the speaking tongue of each family to honor the dead and provide a grand yet intimate farewell. The original Ogham stone was found in County Kerry.

Her pendant clearly was gone from the flat. In all the years she had worn this special gift, she knew it couldn't be too far away. Had Cornelius visited in the night again to play tricks just to have a bit of fun with her and make his presence known?

She hurried to finish her morning ritual, grabbing her corduroy peacoat and gloves. Montreal streets were frosty in late October with the dawn light now filtering down the laneways and illuminating the nineteenth-century brickwork and walk-ups of Rue Jeanne-Mance.

She glanced back one more time before she turned the corner, thinking she had seen a hand waving from behind her front room curtains. Was this his face, his graying hair, once red and thick, now unkempt? Eyebrows bushy and a knowing smile as only she would recognize, his lips full and gentle, the love of kin and a presence she had never known in this lifetime, having lost her birth family at the age of twelve. He was holding his hat in both hands at his waist and wearing a fine suit jacket and tie, looking dapper as only a lifelong bachelor might on a promenade in Dublin.

Would this be one of those days when Cornelius followed her like a friendly shadow, looking over her shoulder while guiding her fingers, correcting the notes that strayed as she played her fiddle riffs for the diminutive students in her class?

*

"We are the barefoot orphan girls," sang the children on cue, "aboard the full-rigged famine ships, / from workhouse o'er the tossing gales / to the shores of New South Wales."[2]

Deirdre called out the chorus for another one of her favorites: "Walk, walk, walk my love. / Walk peacefully and walk quietly. / Walk to the door and escape with me. Siúil, siúil, siúil a rún."[3]

Deirdre disappeared into a daydream and imagined all her charges were pleased and expectant, lining the seats of the music school's main hall, each one a proud member of St. Brigid's patronage: babes and blacksmiths, fugitives and mariners, poets and paupers, sailors and Travellers, and always the waterman in tow. She was their faithful fiddler with open arms for the raucous and the needy. They were her kin now.

The Wrath of *Taranis*

It was the beginning of her twelfth year when Deirdre was tossed into the dark void of a world without family. It had taken her nearly a decade to stop revisiting her old street, Twyford Court, in the district of Islington in Toronto's west suburbs, where her family's home had burned down in the night. Deirdre was the only survivor along with her tabby cat, Roo. She had been plucked from her ordinary life in an extended family of seven, attending public school like all the children on her street, enjoying music lessons every Tuesday with Mr. Ruttledge near Rosethorn Park. Then suddenly she was thrust into the jarring placement in care through the Children's Aid Society. There were no relatives in Canada. Very little was known about the distant family members in County Cork, Ireland. No effort had been made to trace them, and so Deirdre became an orphan and a ward of the crown.

She kept a secret scrapbook ritual after the fire, scribbling all the tales that her Grannie Moll had shared, coloring elaborate maps of the small hamlets of West Cork, knowing that her relatives resided there in the last century. Her foster family was kind, even taking in Roo, but they were strangers to her. They placed a curfew on her lawn concerts and fiddle playing as they said it kept the neighbors agitated.

Not long after her seventeenth birthday, Deirdre ran away with her fiddle, scrapbook, and Ogham pendant. Sadly, Roo had already crossed the rainbow bridge, embarking on his next cat life, having lived twelve days short of his seventeenth year.

Too-ra-loo-ra-loo-ral
Too-ra-loo-ra-li
Too-ra-loo-ra-loo-ral
Hush now, don't you cry.[4]

Good-bye, I'll be seeing you, the lyrics said in Irish—her Grannie Moll humming the lullaby many nights during the electric storms of summer to soothe Diedre's fright as she watched those great arrows of lightning streak down upon the neighborhood through her bedroom window while the hot humid winds of an Ontario storm tore up the roots of her courage. Careless and menacing, the night waged the weather wars of *Taranis*, great god of thunder, lighting, and storms, with cumulonimbus clouds towered across the diminishing sky. This would be followed by ungodly cracks of thunder setting even the china cabinet cups askew and tilting the paintings on the walls. The heavy moist air of those southern Ontario mid-July storms descended like dragon's breath across the darkened horizon.

All it had taken was the wrath of *Taranis* on that fated summer night to throw a lightning fork at the paper birch trees, majestic and adorned within reach of the house. The birch had been Deirdre's favorite tree, sacred to the Celts and thought to have protective influences, foretelling new beginnings. The fire had started so close to the low roofline that it took no time at all before the tinder-dry structure was engulfed in flames.

Diedre's bedroom was close to the back porch and in a flash of instinct and with nightmare speed, she tore towards the backdoor and down the steps to safety. Her parents' and sisters' rooms were down the long hallway, far from the porch, and her grandparents were in the lower-level bedsit. None of them were able to escape. Deirdre was met by a frightened Roo hiding under Grannie Moll's bright yellow forsythia at the corner of the property, narrowly avoiding passage to his ninth and final feline year. He had come to the household several winters before during a January blizzard, all wounded and weary, looking to hang up his feral hat. He never left his living room basket for days until his engine's purr returned with the help of beef medley and cream. Now he was homeless like Deirdre, who clung to him madly until the neighbors rescued them and took them into safety.

She remembered very little about that night, only that Mrs. McLeod next door soothed her with a cup of cocoa, holding it in her shaking hands, and rocking her in a slider chair to sleep, Roo all the while purring and making biscuits on her lap. Beyond that, she had no recollection of the events that followed, including the family's funeral mass or the cards dropped off by schoolmates' families with messages of shock and sorrow. All those cards with their cheery flowers and somber paintings of crosses blurred her vision. A rosary was tucked into an envelope from Miss O'Donnell who lived kitty corner to the house.

Mrs. Alma was assigned to the case. She was a smart Jamaican woman full of heart and a love of children, always speaking with a soothing voice and manner. She had been promoted to the larger district of Etobicoke and took on Diedre's file. It was Mrs. Alma in fact who made all the arrangements for the funeral and burial. Diedre's father James, mother Ella, Grannie Moll and Grampy Llewelyn, her sisters Ruby and Tara, were all gone forever through the fire's flame.

She did not hear anything of the funeral liturgy commending her family to God's mercy and compassion, the recitations at the Rite of Committal which she later read, telling her that death is not the end, nor does it break the bonds forged in life. She had never attended a funeral or encountered death before other than the songbirds and mice she buried in the garden.

That night she fell into a fitful dream, one of many that would follow her through her next decade. What she recalled most vividly in lucid images was the voice of an elderly gentleman, dressed smartly in a suit of light-gray linen, wearing an ivy cap, singing a song that was mostly indistinguishable, holding a fiddle case close to his knees. She only deciphered a few verses and had never heard of Skibbereen:

> O father dear, I oft-times hear you talk of Erin's Isle,
> Her lofty scenes and valleys green, her mountains rude and
> wild.

They say it is a pretty place wherein a prince might dwell.
And why did you abandon it, the reason to me tell."

"Oh it's well I do remember that bleak December day,
The landlord and the sheriff came to drive us all away.
They set my roof on fire with their demon yellow spleen,
And that's another reason why I left old Skibbereen.[5]

Deirdre woke in a fever, lying in the McLeod's guest bed with Roo at her feet. She reached for her Ogham pendant, safely resting on her chest, holding the silver talisman and chain close to her heart while a strange breeze with the scent of sea air flowed through the open window. Where am I, she asked out loud. The sea was more than a thousand miles away, but the saline air was strong. At that moment she did not feel alone. The unmistakable scent of sea spray and marine grasses conjured the many motor trips to Shediac Beach and the Bay of Fundy on family vacations to the east coast. Something had compelled her to sing the opening lines of the song. "O Father dear." . . . Something urged her to invite the gray-haired mystery man to sing with her again.

Who had rescued her fiddle from the flames? Miraculously, there it was resting at the bedside.

Indigo Child

THE TRIFINITY CHILDREN WERE busy in rehearsals each day now that the annual spring concert and St. Anne's Academy fundraiser were just three weeks away. Deirdre would lead her charges in a full recital with several pupils chosen for solo performances. The music was traditional, mixed with more contemporary fiddle airs and reels. She was free to choose her favorites. She had already picked "Auld Lang Syne" and the "Swallow Tail Jig" and was planning Éamon's solo to close the evening program with "Finnegan's Wake".

Éamon was her bright star Rigel in the night sky and no doubt would shine brilliantly at the concert so that he would be accepted as her first-choice applicant for the summer festival in Ireland. Each year the Cork City Arts Council invited young students from many countries to perform and showcase their talents for a potential scholarship to attend Cork College University's Music Department. The program combined scholarship and performance in the study of a diverse range of music traditions from around the world. The young students' program runs alongside the famous annual Cork Folk Festival which would be a once-in-a-lifetime opportunity for young Éamon. If his scores were high enough at the Cork College recital, he would be offered admission to the university once he graduated from high school.

Like many of the children at St. Anne's Academy, Éamon was from a single-mom family with a troubled past. His birth mother, known to him only as Lily O'Connor, had to give him up as a toddler due to unfortunate circumstances including her unabated drug addictions and street life. He had kept her maiden name and one snapshot of her that had been left on the child services file. His foster family had emigrated from Poland to Canada with only their suitcases. Éamon's talent was obvious from the time he was a youngster. His foster parents had always wanted to give the boy a chance to develop his talent in music. He had perfect pitch when he sang, even after hearing the tune only once. He played a tiny electric keyboard they had rescued from a garage sale. Whatever makeshift instrument he picked up, whether it be stones or spoons or strings mounted on a board, he found a rhythm that seemed to flow through his gentle nature.

He was a boy of few words. Although his foster family hardly spoke English, they cared for him deeply and could see he was a special child with advanced wisdom and talent for his age. They sometimes caught him whispering words at bedtime, prayers that did not sound like English, and wondering where he had learned the words or if he had a make-believe world where this secret language was spoken.

Deirdre knew Éamon was gifted when he showed up for his first class and played fiddle like the music was born into him. He played the beautiful air, "The Minstrel Boy" written by Irish poet Thomas Moore, that first day of class. The music poured out from his fiddle through his supple hands. He only had to review the sheet music once to match the sounds perfectly. Deirdre wondered if he came from a musical family, but little was known about Lily or her heritage. It was something that both she and Éamon would no doubt later pursue.

When the concert date arrived, Deirdre spent the morning preparing her introductions, then dressing in her best emerald chemise with sleeves of embroidered burgundy roses and buds. She added her best leather boots to the ensemble which gave her that air of Grannie Moll's style and determination. The boots were very much like the ones in pictures she treasured from the old country, as Moll had named it. She wore her copper curls up in a relaxed bun which accentuated her long neck and slender frame

As expected by her colleagues, it was the tradition for school recitals to have the senior music instructor open the concert with "Miss Kelly's Reel" and close with "The Parting Glass." She had played both many times before and was long over her stage fright, having spent so many years at pub gigs and community halls playing before every kind of audience. When she was with her fiddle, she was lost in her own world of music. The sounds soothed her sadness when the great losses of her short three decades came over her in waves. She was at home with her fiddle and the music filled her with a sense of timelessness, a reprieve that followed her into her dreams.

The concert came and the audience was thrilled. Parents, teachers, siblings, fiddle-aspiring children, and of course the classes from throughout the Academy all attended the concert. Each child managed their instrument so well, so perfectly, with little hands and eyes of innocence. This was their chance to be stars in that one constellation of childhood, not marred by grievances or losses or scoldings. It was their night to believe in possibilities, in happiness and future adventures, unconstrained by family circumstance, fracture, or fate. All things were possible when they stood up on that stage with their fiddles and songs—their feet planted firmly on the oak boards, their true love of music keeping rhythm to their heart's dance, playing all the right notes on beat. Reels, airs, flings, slides, hornpipes—they were playing them all, having learned the intricacies of this musical tradition. This was their night to bring it all together. How special it was to be given this chance.

Éamon came back on stage for the penultimate recital piece—"Finnegan's Wake." Played perfectly, he took a bow and then recited two famous James Joyce lines from the novel:

"They lived and laughed and loved and left. . . . Make me feel good in the moontime."[6] Applause and more applause could be heard throughout the concert hall.

Deirdre wrapped up the evening with "The Parting Glass," encouraging the audience to sing along with the words printed in the concert leaflet.

So fill to me the parting glass
And drink a health whate'er befalls
Then gently rise and softly call
Good night and joy be to you all.[7]

St. Brigid's Blessing

"ÉAMON, CAN YOU COME by today?" Deirdre asked her sleepy-sounding fiddle prodigy as she rang up just before ten. "It's time for us to get going on those Cork College papers and put some pizzazz into your application."

"Yes, Miss Dee," he called her.

Éamon was over to Deirdre's before noon. They sat for hours planning their visit to Ireland, pulling together the best rehearsal recordings, sorting through a few photographs of young Éamon with his Fesley fiddle set, wearing a smart recital outfit. Certainly not the McNeela 4/4 fiddle for advanced students, which he was saving up for with his paper route earnings and tips. It might just be possible to have it before their trip and wouldn't it make all the difference to his sound and destiny, Deirdre thought.

"Éamon, here are the questions they want you to answer. You'll need to describe the differences: the jig, the reel, the horn-pipe, the polka, along with flings, slides, and marches. Then you'll have to sort out each of the sample tunes they post by meter types. Be sure to remind them that many Irish fiddlers emphasize the notes on the beat, but tailor the stress of those notes based on the meter. And finally, you will have to add how you have developed your own traditional lilt and what makes your music different and outstanding."

A tall order for a young lad to answer all these questions of musical theory, especially when all he had to do was pick up the fiddle and play to his heart's content.

"It comes from your blood, not your brain, boy. You have the gift, the Irish streak I'm sure, coming from a line of musical ancestors just like my own Cornelius," said Deirdre. Amen.

The boy was awkward at twelve going on thirteen, often teased because of his petite size compared with classmates. His auburn hair was seldom combed, often falling across his eyes. He had the habit of humming when he was nervous and occasionally murmured a few unintelligible words. Where were these tunes coming from? Deirdre guessed that his first year of life with his mother Lily had been fraught with troubles, scarcity, and with many revolving doors and leaky roofs over his head. At the same time the child carried forth, exhibiting a quiet reserve beyond his years, a keen and introspective spirit.

"Well, a jig is a jig is a jig," he said, "and a reel is more real than a reel! As for the others, I will play you some riffs and I'll be on key."

Deirdre laughed. She loved his cheeky humor but she knew the Academy in Cork would want the correct descriptions written out.

"Go on," she said. "I know you know what they want. Tell me what you've learned in class when the fiddle isn't speaking."

"I love the reels best. They are fast, forward, fun, all in 4/4!" Well, they might be in 4/4—common time, but they are felt in 2/2. The experts call it cut time. I call it my time! The strength is in the 1 and 3 while the tune moves along at a steady clip. Brilliant."

"What else?" Deirdre asked.

"A jig is a jig, but it can be a slip jig or a hop jig—the masters argue the hop is 9/8 but they make more sense in 3/8 with four bars to a part repeated rather than eight. I prefer the slip jig. If you're hearing an extra beat, you're onto the slip jig."

Deirdre was impressed. This discussion went on for quite some time. Éamon was able to differentiate between the flings, slides, the highlands from Donegal and Tyrone, and even the slower set dances. You'd think he'd acquired a photographic memory of *Mel Bay's Complete Irish Fiddle Player* manual. Maybe he did, but most likely she figured it was in the genes. He was a natural. Ancient ears do not forget. Such tunes will always visit in our dreams.

The afternoon light began to grow dim, and they were nearing the finish of their paperwork. Deirdre had made a short video of Éamon playing his best fiddle choice—the "Beare Island Reel"— which they would include in the application. For a refreshment break, Deirdre prepared a pot of Bewley's Gold Blend tea and biscuits which she had baked the evening prior with currents and amaranth. They both indulged in a double pat of butter with the warmed biscuits.

Éamon was quiet after tea and looked preoccupied. He was thinking about his dream of visiting the countryside which until then had only existed in books. The din of Montreal's all day rush-hour streets and markets was all he knew, having never left the inner city's perimeter in all his growing years. A jet plane was like a space bird to him with mighty smoking wings, only encountered in movie theatres or on TV commercials. Three thousand miles in a spaceship where time stopped, he thought. Would he be older when they touched down on the other side? Would he look different, or speak another language? Would he recognize strangers?

Deirdre could see that Éamon's gaze was far away and thought she would bring him back with her own favorite—"St. Brigid's Jig." She played beautifully with passion and a lilt all her own. She longed for Cork, to breathe the ocean air along the Beare Peninsula, to hear the familiar voices of the people of West Cork. She also called for the blessings of St. Brigid to provide them safety on their journey.

Among other things, Brigid was the patron saint of healers and poets as well as creativity and womanhood. Then Deirdre recited the blessing for Éamon:

> *May Brigid bless this house wherein you dwell.*
> *Bless every fireside, every wall and door.*
> *Bless every heart that beats beneath its roof.*
> *Bless every hand that toils to bring it joy.*
> *Bless every foot that walks its portals through.*
> *May Brigid bless the house that shelters you.*[8]

Deirdre leaned over the table and took Éamon's left hand. She knew he was struggling with the prospect of this once-in-a-lifetime chance to make his music known, to take it out into the world, to make it his life and his living. She told him that the next few months would be his chance to prepare, to practice and practice, more and more each day. Together they would send up all their prayers to St. Brigid so that Ireland would be their destination by June's festival.

"Hang on tight to your dreams Éamon," she said. "That is where everything begins."

Éamon's Dream and the Circle of Stones

ÉAMON AWOKE FROM A startling and vivid dream two nights following his visit with Miss Dee when he had worked so hard on his papers for the Cork music recital application. He remembered her saying that he must follow his dreams. This is what he remembered:

There was a circle of stones in a very green field, something the old woman accompanying him called the Drombeg Stone Circle where they could visit the Druid's Altar. The stones all lined up with the setting sun of the summer solstice. Éamon had difficulty speaking his question but finally stuttered it out, "Who is buried there?"

There was a bridge. Was it a railway? Was it for cars? Could people walk across? The old woman named it: The Twelve Arches of Ballydehob. She said it would take us from Skibbereen to Schull on the tramway.

A statue. "The Maid of Erin" was written on a plaque. All the people who had died for Ireland were remembered there. The years of uprisings and great loss were engraved on the pedestal: "1798," "1803," "1848," and "1867." He could see the dates clearly but "1848" was painted red.

There was a doctor there to help the people in the streets. His name was Daniel Donovan. There was a James Mahony from London. He made sketches that were famous. They were very sad sketches.

A sky garden! I could see light, day or night. There were tunnels at the bottom of the oval grassy crater with a stone plinth at its center. It was a peaceful place.

I opened my fiddle case to play a tune when an old man wearing a flat cap and tweeds sat beside me with his tin whistle and sang a verse of this mournful air:

> *You mother, too, God rest her soul, fell on the snowy ground,*
> *She fainted in her anguish, seeing the desolation round,*
> *She never rose, but passed away from life to mortal dream,*
> *And found a quiet grave, my boy, in the Abbey near Skibbereen.*[9]

Éamon woke then, all tangled in his blankets, feeling the rays of sun warming him through the window. It was dawn but barely. He could remember every picture in his dream, every mood and landscape, every word of the song.

"I must tell Miss Dee," Éamon said out loud, then went down the hall hurriedly to phone her.

Deirdre's Dream and the Red Fox

"ÉAMON, WHAT ARE YOU on about? It is half past seven in the morning!" Deirdre was bleary eyed and cranky from a fitful sleep. It was Saturday morning, her time to lie in and catch up on much-needed rest. She was often up late, and no doubt was one of those biphasic sleepers she was always teased about by roommates and her foster folks. She often rested on the couch in the early evening after supper but would come alive after midnight—her time to read and jot down phrases in her diary, things that stood out from her day and from the poetry she was always reading. She even recorded a few stanzas of her own, but these were secret and off-limits to all. She never considered herself a poet.

Her diary had been nicked in grade eleven by a bratty boy who had a crush on her. He had hidden it in a vacant locker, but she was convinced that the whole school had read it. Deirdre was mortified, forgetting that most people couldn't possibly read her left-handed scrawl. She marched to the principal's office to complain and threatened to quit classes altogether over the matter. It was an issue of privacy and rights, she had declared. She would not learn a thing in such an errant establishment as this dumb school. It was only a few days later when Marnie, her biology lab schoolmate, gingerly placed the diary on her desk. It looked a bit more ragged but there it was in front of her. Marnie never confessed how she had found it.

Deirdre had already decided to quit high school and continued to plot her exit. As soon as her sixteenth birthday arrived, she could walk away without the truant officer's interference, but she decided to finish up the term while planning her escape. She had no idea how she would flee from her foster family with only twenty dollars in her pocket. She would get a job in a bookshop at the plaza or maybe in the ice cream shop on weekends. One of the two stores would snatch her up, she was certain.

"OK, OK, OK, Éamon, settle yourself down, speak more slowly, tell me more. Sounds like your dream was a magical interlude, something of importance. Likely a bit of time travel. Maybe you've been looking at picture books of Ireland?"

"No Mam, I don't have time for those books between fiddle practice and my paper route. The people and the places were so real. I was certain I had been there before. Tell me, can we go to that west corner of Cork to be sure?"

Éamon then began to describe the images that came to him in his dream. Each one was vivid, haunting, familiar and unfamiliar at the same time. Deirdre listened closely to each one of his descriptions. She knew that he had a visitor of some importance who had come to him in the night. She wasn't sure how this related to their planned trip to Cork for his recital. She needed more clues. She reassured him that this was very good news, and he was certainly meant to take this journey. Secretly she wondered if old Cornelius was playing a part, on the move again, showing them the way, urging both to uncover their family ties with Ireland.

The next day being Sunday was her weekly constitutional along the Canal de l'Aqueduc to spend the afternoon in Parc Angrignon, counting all the species of birds she might see near the pond: little blue heron, harlequin ducks, pied-billed grebe, crows and ravens of course, purple martin, killdeer, indigo bunting. If she stayed the whole day the list would grow.

Deirdre tired herself out enough walking home that afternoon and went to bed early, just after midnight. Her dream woke her in a cold sweat at exactly 4:44 a.m. What she remembered was projected in stark, photographic images, monotone like the old silent movies that Grandpa Llewellyn had shown her. This is what she recalled:

*Fire flames rage behind windows and doors. The mosaic patterns of shattered glass. She runs and runs, then discovers Roo has died and she wants to bury him. She struggles through overgrown fields to find the cat cemetery. There is a sign with only one direction pointing west. When she arrives at the burial grounds there are feral cats in the brambles watching her. They form a circle. When she digs Roo's grave, she finds the bones of another cat in the shallow earth. She moves on so as not to disturb the remains and digs another plot. The same thing happens over and over again. She cannot find an inch of ground where there are no skeletons. She finally retreats under the single Hawthorn tree she spots at the far end of the field and there she buries Roo. She plays to him a mournful air as best she can with her woeful hands—"*Port na bPúcaí*"—song of the spirits from the Blaskets. As she concludes her music, she looks up to see a red fox—the only color in her dream—moving along at a lope gait through the tall grass, barely visible. He is making his way to the sea, so the music tells her.*

Bonna Night, Leaping Through Flames

"ARE YOU READY?" DEIRDRE quizzed Éamon after class, the last gathering of the Trifinity students before the summer break.

"Sure am, Miss Dee," Éamon spoke confidently. "When can we start our packing?"

The flight to Dublin would leave the week before summer solstice. They would be nicely settled in at Cobh for the opening of the festival which coincided with one of the oldest traditions in Cork, *Tine Cnáimh* (fire of bones)—Bonna Night, held each year in June on St. John's Eve. This Celtic celebration goes back to pagan times, honoring the goddess Áine, who was sometimes depicted as a red mare and was even thought to be a fairy queen. Áine was the goddess of summer, for her very name translates to "brightness," ensuring a bountiful harvest. Bonfires are lit all over the countryside along with singing, dancing, and prayer.

To prove their bravery, the young men at Bonna Night would leap through the flames. To bless the ground for a healthy harvest, weeds from garden and fields would be burnt and the ashes would then be scattered on the land.

"Éamon, will you be leaping through the bonfires too?" Deirdre teased.

"Yes I will!" Éamon declared, wanting to be the bravest and best fiddler in the Trifinity class.

Deirdre gave him a list of what to bring on the trip. She wanted to keep it simple and avoid the usual laments of lost luggage that often occurred with overseas flights. She handed a note to Éamon:

"Other than the clothes on your back and the good sturdy shoes you wear on the flight, this is all you will need: 2 pairs of trousers, one fancy; 2 shirts, one white for your recital; notebook and beeswax candle; your good luck charm (keep it in your pocket at all times); your fiddle and case: guard with your life on the plane; don't forget the sheet music. All of this should fit in one rucksack, easy to carry. Tie a red ribbon on the handle."

Ó hAodha Family Circle

DEIRDRE KNEW THAT THE trip to Ireland would shine light on the mysteries around her Cork ancestry and Great-Grandfather, Cornelius. She had been searching for clues for years and had never been able to track down the parish records or confirm extended family members through all her years of genealogy research. Deirdre had learned that the volumes held at the Public Records Office of Ireland were destroyed by fire during the Battle of Dublin in 1922, including seven centuries of archives: records for all baptisms, marriages, and burials. She had even taken the DNA test which led to a number of false starts, but she remained hopeful that this trip would provide her with answers, or at least closure.

She joined the Ó hAodha Family Circle of West Cork and corresponded with them regularly. Their group chair, Siobhan Byrne, knew she was coming in June and set up a meeting with the members to take place in Skibbereen. Deirdre was certain that all the synchronicities of late, sometimes in the form of sightings behind window curtains or the occasional line of poetry on handwritten notes and found in library books, were deliberate and that Cornelius was trying to share something with her. Her missing Ogham pendant, however disconcerting, was another clue, warning that she must follow her instincts and fall into resonance with the land next to the Celtic Sea. The opportunity to visit Ireland in June was possible only through Éamon's brilliance and musical talent, along with the generous sponsorship of St. Anne's Academy and the Cork College University. She knew that this journey would bring lasting peace, along with a deeper wisdom that would illuminate her way.

Cornelius Comes Calling

DEIRDRE GOT UP QUICKLY from the sofa where she had fallen asleep after supper. She heard three loud knocks on the door at the bottom of the narrow stairwell leading to her apartment.

"Who's calling at this hour?" she spoke through the door. No answer. Uneasy and aware of neighborhood pranksters, she did not want to open the door unless she heard a reassuring voice, maybe Éamon's or one of her other students wishing her well for the trip, just two days away. She gave up waiting for a friendly voice and fastened the chain lock to the door.

Not long after she heard another knock, this time from the kitchen porch where she often sat for her evening cup of tea on warm summer evenings. The door had a light curtain and not much of a lock, but she was three stories up and it would not be easy for an intruder to climb that brick wall to the landing. She turned out her kitchen lights and peered out the window. Nothing, no one in sight. Incandescent light from apartments across the laneway shone through the beveled glass. A regal-looking tabby cat, sporting a good twenty pounds with ample girth, sat content on the landlord's ledge next door. Maybe it was the trellis for her porch garden tomato plants tapping against the window. Clearly no one was there knocking. She gave up worrying and ran a bath. She would relax and try for an early night, not an easy feat with such a busy mind.

She lay awake for what felt like weeks and then fell into a half-sleep. The night sky was bright and clear with a waxing gibbous moon. Deirdre then dropped further into what seemed a lucid dream, complete with images clear as day inviting all her senses.

First, she noticed the strong aroma of a tobacco pipe. She had learned that a typical Irish brand popular the 1880s was Peterson's Irish Flake, possibly what old Cornelius smoked in his clay pipe.

One of her fiddle-playing friends from her gigging days who smoked a pipe would tell her, "Quite frankly Peterson's was made exclusively for the full-scrotum crowd. Delicious, strong, and cool burning. A fresh sweet natural tobacco but very deep with high octane nicotine." Yes, she thought, this would be Cornelius's favorite pipe tobacco. I'll look for it when I'm there, she figured.

Then she felt a breezy wash of sea air move through the room along with the scent of a slow burning peat fire. She knew that aroma from her visit to the Aran Islands those years ago where peat fires heated all the island cottages. She had brought a small piece home with her and took in that rich scent like rare incense from the earth.

Her hands felt the texture of worsted wool, rustic and strong, likely a men's flat cap left out in the damp air following a spring rain, made from long-staple pasture wool spun from the Galway sheep. She would look for such a perfect cap for Éamon.

Then Deirdre tasted a hint of Guinness on her tongue. With that rich roasted aroma and the hue of midnight ruby, it was a drink she had often ordered while standing in for fiddle at Hurley's on Crescent Street. Once prescribed as an iron tonic, it is a blend of malted barley, hops, yeast, and water, and is said to contain protective plant compounds for excellent health. She remembered Grannie Moll giving it to Grampy when he was feeling low and achy.

Deirdre was slipping into a deeper well of sleep when she heard a man's voice reciting lines from a poem, something the voice called "The Silver Mistress of our Dreams":

> *I walked out in the night air, all holly and hazel with crisp inhalations,*
> *the shaggy flock of Cheviot ewes startled by my rustling presence*
> *having felt a figure pass before in mid-evening clarity.*

All manner of songbirds nesting in hidden crooks and
corners
near-light fallen to the lee of the glen, on the southern bank
a leaning tree misshapen with age and wind's restlessness
waits for the moon's final repose . . .[10]

Deirdre woke then, startled by familiar words and images, the very stanza she had found, scribbled on the note that was tucked in her library book that day—a copy of Grave's *The White Goddess*—of birth, love, and death, and the mythic source of poetry.

She then gave up on sleep and sat down at her desk, reaching for her journal to write out all that she had encountered. She even tried to sketch the figure that she had seen behind the curtain. "Is that you, Cornelius?" she called out impatiently, wishing for more sleep and reassurance. His visitations were making her more sleepless and longing for connection. As she turned back to bed, she felt the slight brush of his sleeve against her left cheek. The scent of pipe tobacco was unmistakable.

PART TWO

Going Home

Do we distill to passion
after centuries of loss?
Is this our new language,
the knowing field?
Ogham's mystery stones,
mapping the journey home.[11]

—DIANA HAYES, FROM "NOTATIONS ON A MAP"

Deirdre's Well of Sorrows

ÉAMON COULDN'T CONTAIN HIS animated spirits while they boarded their great silver jumbo jet to London, then onto the smaller Aer Lingus bird, all green and white with a shamrock on its tail, connecting them to Dublin at last. He hardly sat still the entire trip, getting up to peer out windows from both aisles of the plane at the vast body of land and water so far below, cruising at thirty-eight thousand feet. The screen in front of his seat traced the flight route and location of the plane at each stage of travel. He kept peering at the monitor to keep track of all the places they passed over: first, Quebec City and the Gaspé, then a small island called L'Île d'Anticosti, a protected area Deirdre described as remote and abundant with diverse fossil fauna from the first mass extinction of animal life.

"How many years ago did the animals disappear?" asked Éamon, not able to grasp the concept of extinction.

"Well over 400 million years ago," Deirdre told him as he squiggled his forehead in an expression of disbelief, trying to imagine what sounded to him like eons, or infinity as his science teacher had once tried to explain.

The next point of land on the screen was the bottom tip of Labrador, then what felt like long boring hours crossing the Atlantic.

"How long would it take to sail these seas by ship?" Éamon asked.

Deirdre disappeared into a dark vision of the coffin ships, crossing to Canada from Queenstown—the Cove of Cork, now known as Cobh. The poorly built sailing vessels took between six and eight weeks to complete the crossing to Canada but depending on the weather, it could take up to twelve weeks. No less than one in five survived the journey, either perishing en route or dying of the fever—typhus—when they landed at the immigration depot and quarantine at La Grosse-Île in the St. Lawrence. The Grosse-Île cemetery was the largest burial grounds for refugees from the Great Hunger outside of Ireland.

"Well, you can certainly cross in today's world in seven nights on a cruise ship," Deirde told him, "but the cost is dear, well over two thousand dollars for a single one-way fare during the month of June."

Their arc of travel continued to be displayed on Éamon's monitor. Eventually their jet would cross over land again just above the northern coast of Inishbofin in County Galway, then across through the middle of Ireland before flying over the Irish Sea en route to London.

By the time they boarded their connecting flight to Dublin at Heathrow, they had been in and out of airports or in the air for over ten hours. It would only take this last leg of travel back across the Irish Sea and soon they would settle into the Sandymount in Dublin. Lucky for them, a patron of the Cork Music Festival sponsored their accommodations while in the country and the Sandymount would be a central and elegant Dublin stay.

Just as the plane circled Dublin airport preparing for landing, Deirdre felt a wave of deep sadness and anticipation. This was not her first trip to Ireland, having landed a summer gig when she was twenty-five, playing fiddle in Kinsale and Cobh with a few of her music mates from Montreal. She had that same overwhelming rush of emotion when she had arrived the first time. Just as the wheels touched down, she spotted a husk of hares in the fields beyond the runway. They were native to Ireland and thought to be mystical animals associated with magic, the Otherworld, and the moon. Tears welled up. She had a hard time concealing her grief from Éamon.

"What is it Miss Dee, why are you crying?"

How to begin to tell Éamon the story of her heart's grief, the well of sadness that followed her on every journey and into her darkest dreams at night. Would she reveal the violent flames of fire that took her family, and thereafter her perpetual search for kin and kinship for which she yearned?

"Éamon, I will tell you more about the well of sorrows as we make our way down to Cork and as our journey unfolds."

She drifted off into recollections of a play she studied about her namesake, *Deirdre of the Sorrows*, and the fated maiden's betrothal to the High King of Ulster. The young woman was aware of the druid's prophecy that she would be the doom of the sons of Usna and ultimately take her own life, using her beloved Naisi's dagger. Deirdre had attended the three-act play written by Irish playwright John Millington Synge at the theater when she first arrived in Dublin those years ago. She could not release that desperate image from her mind, the play's finale when Deirdre falls into Naisi's open grave.

As a child, Deirdre puzzled over her name which she wasn't particularly fond of it. She preferred Dorothy or Daphne. She figured there must have been reason for her parents to name her after that ill-fated, headstrong Celtic heroine who believed it was better to die young, at the peak of love, than to grow old in the shadows of her idyllic past.

Finally, they disembarked at Dublin airport and went straightaway to the New Way Car Hire booth. They drove off to the Sandymount Hotel, an easy twenty minutes into the city, where they were booked for their first night.

It was the end of day when they arrived with just enough energy to have a small meal before settling in for much-needed sleep.

For bedtime reading to Éamon, Deirdre opened a favorite poetry book by David Whyte, and began his poem, "The Well of Grief":

Those who will not slip beneath
  the still surface on the well of grief,
turning down through its black water
  to the place we cannot breathe . . .[12]

Éamon interrupted, asking Deirdre where exactly was this well of sorrow she described when they touched down in Dublin. He asked again why she was crying as the plane landed.

Remembering her namesake's seven years in exile with Naisi at their idyllic place of refuge at the Scottish Loch Etive—believed to mean *little fierce one*—she sighed, wondering how she could explain to Éamon the many layers that are contained in the well's turbid history, the collective grief that all Irish souls must carry. She continued, revealing the essence of the story, painting the closing images in words from Synge's *Deirdre of the Sorrows*.

The mythic Deirdre, daughter of a royal storyteller, was snatched from her parents by the Ulster King and brought up in seclusion by Lavarcham, a poet and wise woman. The King's chief Druid prophesied that she would grow up to be exceptionally beautiful, and that kings and lords would go to war over her.

"Going to war over beauty?" Éamon asked with that quizzical expression he often wore.

In Synge's play, the poet and wise woman tells of Deirdre's fate when she is returned to the king. Both she and her lover Naisi are dead, *and if the oaks and stars could die for sorrow, it's a dark sky and a hard and naked earth we'd have this night in Emain.*[13]

"Look deep into the well and hear the old stories rise up with each salty tear," Deirdre said. "The Banshee's tears foretold of sorrows too, but our tears contain the alchemy for healing and can soothe our broken hearts."

Deirdre then read the closing lines from Whyte's poem as Éamon was drifting off to sleep:

will never know the source from which we drink,
  the secret water, cold and clear,
nor find in the darkness glimmering,
  the small round coins,
    thrown by those who wished for something else.[14]

Walking to Joyce's Tower

THE NIGHT DISTINCTLY FELT like it was still day, with time zones askew, and Deirdre thought it was actually morning. They slept fitfully and dreamless as most folks complain when jet-lagged, but they rose early for a full Irish breakfast at the hotel's Whitty's. Their plan was to walk the Sandymount Strand and visit Grafton Street later for a midday meal before heading off to Glendalough in the Wicklow Mountains. It was only a few hours' drive to where they were booked in at Derrybawn House in Laragh. From there, it was close enough for them to walk the green road all the next day and explore Glendalough, the medieval monastic settlement founded by St. Kevin, known as *Cóemgen*.

St. Kevin's dream was to find his god in solitude and prayer. His hermitage was secluded above the shore of Glendalough's Upper Lake. He had a love of birds and all of nature while living a lonely, devotional life. Deirdre thought that Éamon would find *Cóemgen's* place of solitude the perfect surroundings for relaxation before his recital the coming weekend. They would both need to look inward and prepare mentally for what was ahead.

It was said by those who wrote of *Cóemgen* that "the branches and leaves of the trees sometimes sang sweet songs to him, and heavenly music alleviated the severity of his life."[15] It was in his diminutive cave dwelling where St. Kevin learned to play the harp. The very harp he played is a relic now kept at the Glendalough Museum. Deirdre imagined they would hear distant sounds of harp music from their Derrybawn rooms. They would take the

39

green road early the next morning and start out just before sunrise to visit the Upper Lake and to feel *Cóemgen*'s solitude, the mystical air of the Glen of Two Lakes, the *genius loci*.

Deirdre and Éamon set off for the Sandymount Strand coastal path where they took their much-needed constitutional. All those hours in airports and on planes left them with heavy legs and fuzzy minds. Farther along they reached the Great South Wall and walked another good stretch with views of the Poolbeg Lighthouse, with Howth and Dún Laoghaire in the distance. They even spotted seals and dolphins breaching in Dublin Bay as they walked the strand. They would reach Sandycove Point finally to see the James Joyce Tower, which Deirdre knew was the opening setting for Joyce's *Ulysses*.

Deirdre had struggled with reading Joyce's books. She had ventured through *Ulysses* many times, but her true Joyce moment was discovering *Finnegan's Wake* with its even more dreamlike style, word punning, and radical inventions with language; the way that memories, people, and places appear as if through the veil of a half-awakened consciousness, allowing the subconscious mind the freedom to roam. She wondered if Joyce's baffling words and phrases related to the secret Gammon of her ancestors, that hidden language meant only for Travellers' ears. *Finnegan's Wake* was Joyce's most difficult book, leaving readers lost at the time of its publication.

There were buskers along the strand and Éamon was sorry he hadn't brought along his fiddle so he could join in. A tall young man in a flap cap was playing the uilleann pipes and two other boys in their teens were playing tin whistle. The music was lovely, the first they had heard since landing in Dublin. Éamon called it the old country after reading the phrase at school many times, imitating a lilted accent. An echo of Grannie Moll's expression.

"Did you know Éamon, that lovely little cap he is wearing was once mandatory garb—apparently to ensure a prosperous wool market in England—many centuries ago. Young boys had to wear those caps on Sundays and holidays, starting at the age of six years. It caught on so well that it became a symbol of the working class, farmers, and tradesmen and this tradition continued to this day, even though the Queen's foolish law was repealed twenty years after it was declared."

The fresh sea air and exercise made them both hungry. They walked back at a good pace and reached Bewley's on Grafton Street in time for early afternoon tea, a plate of local cheeses and smoked meats, some of the finest they were told even by Dubliners.

The road trip to Glendalough and Laragh would take just over two hours if they got away by midafternoon. Deirdre knew that the drive through the majestic Wicklow Mountains and farther on to Derrybawn House would conjure a deep sense of returning, a magnetic pull towards Cork and the Celtic Sea where her heart would beat stronger and steadier, bringing a sense of reunion, a place of belonging. It was this innate knowing that came with intergenerational memories, along with abiding instincts that gave her the Traveller's touch with the fiddle and strong feet for the journey.

Valley of the Glen of the Waterfall

IT WAS JUST BEFORE three o'clock when Deirdre and Éamon set off from Dublin in their Volkswagen Polo to Laragh Village by way of the Sally Gap. The starting point was the Old Military Road, built by the British Army after the 1798 Irish Rebellion, leading directly into the heart of the Wicklow Mountains. Deirdre remembered the stunning views accented with carpets of vibrant purple heather and blanket bogs. She had taken this route on her previous trip and had even clipped a few sprigs of heather, still tucked in her journal, planting the intention for her return.

They could make a few stops along the way to breathe in the clear mountain air and relax. Lough Tay and the majestic cascade of Glenmacnass Waterfall were certainly imprinted in her mind's eye and were familiar watermarks for what lay ahead. Happily, they were not pressed for time to arrive at Laragh Village.

Éamon had his head buried in the guide map when they turned at the Old Military Road. The way then became winding and solitary with a scatter of darkening clouds overhead, and hardly any cars on the road. Not unusual conditions for June, this was Deirdre's preferred weather for road trips and journeys on foot.

"Miss Dee, the guidebook says Lough Tay looks like a pint of Guinness!"

"Well, that will make us thirsty for sure," Deirdre said, knowing that even twelve-year-old boys, going on thirteen as was Éamon, were allowed to have the odd half-pint of Guinness for good health while in Ireland. "All those vitamins, Éamon, will make your fiddling stronger for the Cork recital!"

Lough Tay was in fact famous for the Guinness look, with its peaty waters and white sandy beach, making it appear like an overflowing pint of stout; a dark broody liquid with its newly poured, surging white froth, spilling over the glass and onto the shores. A bit of a stretch she thought, but lyrical certainly as landscape always has the last dance with the beholder.

"What about the waterfall, Miss Dee? What makes it so special?

"Well, it's old, very old like the valley itself, dating back to the Ice Age. There is even evidence of moraines in the area—boulder-strewn mounds, marking the positions of the ice front and running right across the valley."

"I love how the names sound in English," he added. "Valley of the Glen of the Waterfall." It made him think of those passages he had to memorize for church services, a psalm he recalled, saying something about the Valley of the Shadow of Death, but this time he was pleased it was water and not death. All those somber hours spent on hard bench pews in dank stone buildings—he remembered them too often. It scared him and he didn't understand the Latin words anyway, along with his foster family muttering the phrases in Polish: *Dolina Cienia Śmierci*. What would it be in Irish, he wondered out loud.

"*Gleann Scáth an Bháis*," Deirdre answered, remembering only because she has learned the Irish words in defiance of the church. She had discovered a beautiful musical rendition of Psalm 23 called "*Sé an Tiarna m'Aoire*" by cellist Ilse de Ziah, who now lived in Cork, and had adapted it for her fiddle. There had been too many hours spent in catechism classes after church when all she wanted to do was get home to play fiddle and read to Roo.

When they arrived at Lough Tay, the clouds had set in and there was a light mist hovering above the lake. They decided to push on to the waterfall and there they would take a pause for refreshments. Deirdre had bought some buns and cheese at Bewley's to add to a bar of chocolate along with sodas. They would have a picnic to revive their energy for the last leg of their trip to Laragh.

Conjuring the image of a waterfall became Deirdre's comfort, her escape when she felt too sad for words, empty of music, especially during those first years after the fire. Everything had gone dark for her then. Days, seasons, years; all the distance between became indistinguishable, merely a shadow of a home that once was—a place and time she would not let herself call up very often, if at all.

There had been a family trip to the Canyon Sainte-Anne Falls, not far from Old Quebec in the Canadian Shield. Standing on the suspension bridge, high above the river and not far along from the falls, she heard the surging roar and felt a mist of cooling water kissing her face. Grannie Moll was holding her hand, sharing the power of water and exhilaration with her. She never forgot that moment and returned to it often in her dreams.

They arrived at the parking area for Glenmacnass and pulled up at the top of the hill, gathering their picnic things into a small rucksack for the short walk along the grassy verge. They could see a small bench with a perfect vantage point closer to the falls. They could hear the water getting louder as they approached. The falls were recorded at eighty meters over the edge at the head of the Glenmacnass Valley, a little higher than the Sainte-Anne Falls, and both being tiered. Deirdre felt it was tamer here, not a wild roar but a steady accelerating pitch of busy water. They were not able to get close enough to feel the mist rising from the tumbling flow as there were safety fences and stone walls, preventing access closer to the edge, so they settled on their bench.

Deirdre knew it was time to share with Éamon more about her quest to find her lost family in West Cork. She did not want to distract him from his music practice before their trip, but once they were landed in Ireland, she knew he would be inquisitive and would want to understand her longings for the old country.

"Éamon, the waterfall is the best place to look for the invisible, to visit the Otherworld, or *Annwn* as the Celts named it. I want to share my story of Cornelius, my great-grandfather, with you."

Deirdre went on to tell him that Cornelius was a Traveller from West Cork; a tinker, a fine tin whistle player, loquacious in the Gammon, a proud Ó hAodha, born in 1823 in Skibbereen Union, Cork. By the time *An Gorta Mór* was at its worst, the Great Hunger at its most murderous stages especially in County Cork, Cornelius was without caravan and horse, penniless, emaciated, and looking to stowaway to England as did many families escaping the famine. Many of his family members perished by starvation no doubt, or from all the colors of disease: black for typhus, yellow for relapsing fever, blue for cholera, laying together now and forever with overlapping bones in the famine pits at Abbeystrowry. It was believed by Deirdre's father that Cornelius escaped, hiding aboard on one of the coffin ships—perhaps Bright Maeve—from Cobh, named then as Queensland, sailing across to St. David's, Wales. By a miracle he made it across the roiling seas, her father was certain. Deirdre had been searching for Cornelius since she was first told of his story by her family. She was only able to trace a few details from documents found in the Southwark archives and in the parish registry in Richmond, Surrey, where he lived his final year, but she was convinced there was more to his story and there were descendants of the family still living in Ireland. Her determination was stalwart, and she was dogged in her research. Nothing would keep her from learning the truth about her family of origin. She was always looking for signs and when her Ogham pendant went missing in the spring, she knew it was time to return to Cork. She was closer to solving the mystery than ever.

Éamon listened intently to Deirdre's story and never uttered a word. He had always wondered about her family. She never spoke of anyone, least of all her parents. He stayed quiet. She didn't tell him about the visitations, how Cornelius would appear sometimes at her flat back on Rue Jeanne-Mance, how he spoke to her in riddles or verse, and always with a friendly demeanor.

On the walk back to the car, Deirdre told Éamon the last details of her family loss in Ontario. She spoke of the lightning storm and the fire, and without saying much more she finished with the miracle of Roo and her fiddle; how they escaped the fire, beyond explanation and at all odds. Éamon remained quiet. His only remark was to ask if her family visited in her dreams now and if she still cried a lot.

Deirdre was tired from the long day and especially from the fierce emotions stirred up from the stories she shared, the family grief ever-present. They packed up their picnic things and carried on with the final lap on the Sally Gap to their lodgings at Laragh before dusk. It was less than a week before the summer solstice so there was light long into the evening.

Derrybawn and the House Sparrow

DERRYBAWN HOUSE WOULD BE their lodgings for two nights while exploring Glendalough and the lake trails. They were due in Cork City by the end of the week to check in and register for the music festival and then settle in at their hotel in Cobh.

Derrybawn was known for its elegant wisteria-clad exterior, cut-stone and brick-built house, with a nineteenth-century Italian design, giving the ninety-three-acre property the feel of a rolling Tuscan hillside. Set back well from the road and only minutes from the village of Laragh, it was ideal for visitors as it linked directly to the green road which would be their pathway to the Glendalough monastery site and the lakes.

Éamon, always reading and curious about his surroundings, had found a pamphlet on Derrybawn that spoke of the Celtic Tiger—*An Tíogar Ceilteach.*

"Will we be seeing tigers here, Miss Dee?" he questioned.

"It is complicated, Éamon, and certainly we won't be seeing tigers!" Deirdre had stayed at the guest house at its peak during her previous visit, but sadly it had fallen into disrepair due to the "The Boom" coming to a crash, ending Ireland's "Economic Miracle," sometimes referred to as the Celtic Tiger. Although Derrybawn was nothing like its original lavish guest house, it was still the perfect location and had been arranged for them by one of the festival committee's members, a relative of the Dowlings, now the new owners. They had spent untold funds on refurbishing the building, bringing it back from its sorry state of abandonment.

"What is a strongroom, Miss Dee? The pamphlet boasts that there is a hidden place next to the master's bedroom." Éamon was fascinated with the details of Derrybawn and when they finally arrived, he couldn't wait to explore the entire building with all its elaborate rooms.

"A strongroom is where you store special things like money and jewelry. There would be a safe in the small room with combination locks and all. Maybe even a shotgun!" she added, adding intrigue to her description.

It was past eight when they settled in their rooms. Luckily, the concierge insisted on ringing the kitchen to provide them with what she called a light tea, given the hour, which ended up being a poached Atlantic salmon fillet with fresh vegetables from the garden and Irish apple cake for dessert. After all that fresh air from their day trip through the Wicklow Mountains, they were ready for a hot meal.

After tea, Deirdre browsed through a field guide while they sat in the great room before turning in at bedtime. It was all about the birds she hoped to see the next day at Glendalough—starling, wood warbler, Eurasian jay, and Sparrowhawk would certainly accompany them on their walks, but what about the goldfinch, one of the most colorful garden birds in Ireland? She also read that the goldfinch symbolized redemption, healing, resurrection, and the soul in Italian art. Possibly death and sacrifice too, but still resurrection would always follow. Their walk would take them along pathways through woodlands and there would be sections of open fields. The list of birds appearing in the month of June was long as noted in birders' records. Deirdre hoped she would also see the fast and agile Sparrowhawk with its russet cheeks, speckled underwings, and gray striped chest feathers.

What about St. Kevin's blackbird, she wondered? Would they spot it above the Upper Lake where his sleeping cell was situated? Deirdre was always watching out and listening for ravens and crows at home. Would St. Kevin's blackbird croak in Irish, or maybe the Cant? Was the bird one of St. Kevin's miracles?

At bedtime, she read her entry from her old journal, *Gleann Dá Loch*, to Éamon. She told him about the house sparrow that had hopped up the stone stairs in front of her as she climbed up to St. Kevin's Cell.

"The house sparrow carries the souls of the deceased to heaven," she told him. "Kevin was considered the Irish St. Francis and loved all animals. He had the gift to heal even the birds."

> *Upon the Wishing Cross he would bare his desire, his spirit heavy with self-confinement, but not in this small world did he gather the vision of beasts, for while aloft in remote banks of the great Lough, patterns became creations, ripples on the glass water grew like chasms in his heart . . .*
>
> *. . . for in his cell he reached beyond the greed and battlements of the Tower, his own footing hewn in simple steps, circular to the landing, no roof or shelter to take his attention but upward, reaching, breathless, toward the sparrow's arcing flight.*[16]

Glendalough and St. Kevin's Cell

DEIRDRE WOKE TO LIVELY birdsong through the garden windows that were set ajar for morning air. She spotted grebes and tufted ducks and mallards, all manner of water birds enjoying the early sun on the pond just beyond the courtyard below, although it was the familiar song and chatter of the Barn Swallow, the *Fáinleog*, she heard coming from under the wide eaves of the garden cottage close to house. There she spotted the distinctive mud nests high up and tucked into the corner cladding next to the roof. It was the familiar witt-witt-witt sounds repeated in endless succession to form the sweet twitter crescendo that was so joyful and had been the harbinger of warmer days. Those bright red faces, appearing sunburned she thought, along with the contrast of blue-black feathers with their unique forked tail that made them look like enchanted faery birds as they twirled and swooped over the lawns. She took this warm avian welcome to be a good omen for the day ahead.

Éamon was sleepy-headed and quiet at breakfast and she had a hard time getting a word out of him. She wondered if her talk of lost families and tragic fire the day before had given him a troubled night. The day would bring them both on a welcome hike in the forests and fields along the Wicklow Way to Glendalough. After all those long hours sitting on planes and in the car, she was certain the extra two days ahead of their arrival in Cork would set them up nicely for a fresh start at the festival. She planned a run-through on fiddle with Éamon that evening to review his repertoire for the recital after they returned to Derrybawn House.

They set out with snacks in a satchel and enough water to drink for the day. The skies were clear. Both Éamon and Deirdre were open to the day's discoveries. Deirdre had spent considerable time studying St. Kevin, paying close attention to details of his healing powers and love of nature. He lived as a hermit in a partially man-made cave, a small and narrow cell known as St. Kevin's Bed. Angels had led him there, so it was said, and he went barefoot, eating nettles and herbs and spending many hours in prayer. Knowing this made Deirdre feel less alone, less afraid of what she might find when she uncovered the truth about her Irish family. Would Kevin's harp sooth her restlessness? Would he absolve her from the anguish at being torn from her home through the flames?

"Our holy inner fire requires the kindling of our vision, the tinder of our imagination, and the fuel of the numinous. Fire can awaken us to the Mysteries of Spirit."[17] This she had read in a book about St. Kevin and wrote it out in full to remember in her journal.

As they passed the centuries-old oak forest along the lower slopes of Derrybawn Mountain, they came upon the monastic enclosure with its enormous Round Tower, thirty-three meters in height, with its conical roof intact. The plaque on the tower wall read that the roof had to be replaced in 1876 when it was struck by lightning. The name for the tower was *Cloigtheach*, meaning "bell tower," but it was sometimes used as a place of refuge for the monks when they were under attack, serving as a lookout post and beacon.

Éamon became animated at the sight of the Round Tower, asking if they could climb to the top.

"No, unfortunately it isn't allowed," Deirdre told him. "They would have entered using a ladder. The entrance door is up three and a half meters and we couldn't climb up without steps."

"Too bad we didn't pack a rope ladder, one of those three-story types they sell back home at Canadian Tire, or even the kind they use off the stern of a boat," Éamon added, knowing a little bit about rope ladders from his afternoon visits with Big Brothers at the community center where they were always talking about safety and being prepared for anything and everything.

"Yes," Deirdre sighed, knowing that Éamon was much more interested in climbing the tower than visiting St. Kevin's Bed.

"Well then what about the lizards, will we get to see them at the lakeside?" he asked.

Deirdre was not fond of lizards or any reptiles for that matter, especially if they frequented lakes. She hoped the creatures would not appear, but the tourist signs directed visitors to cross over to the other side by the bridge where they would find the lake edge and lizards basking on the rocks in the sun. Dragonflies would also be seen in static swarms. Just as they stepped away from the boardwalk, closer to the marshy wetlands, they spotted blue hawker dragonflies by the dozen, circling and darting, flying backwards and forwards with alacrity and dazzle. No lizards yet, but Éamon went on a search. Later, he would beg Deirdre to let him capture one and bring it along to Cork in his kit bag. Not going to happen, she said to herself, but luckily Éamon came up empty-handed. He tried lunging towards one of the brownish-green lizards but all too quickly it made a dash under the boardwalk.

"He had black stripes down his back and a very long tail," Éamon said, sounding sad that he had missed his chance to capture what was known simply as the common lizard, Ireland's only native reptile, dating back to the last Ice Age.

"He would have shed his tail rather than join you on your sojourn to Cork!" Deirdre laughed, knowing the little creature would not have survived the trip.

*

The guidebook directed them to climb the steps at the back of the Reefert Churchyard and follow the path to the west. At the top of a rise overlooking the Upper Lake, the scant remains of St. Kevin's Bed, a small beehive hut, would be found.

But first, Deirdre insisted they walk the Graveyard Trail where many headstones were half-fallen, names mostly illegible.

The oldest graves were situated near the east gable of the Priests' House; grave slabs with no names dating from the eleventh century. The oldest marked stone had the name Murlaugh Doyle inscribed, 1697.

Farther along, in the adjacent churchyard were graves from the mid-1800s, some from the time of the Great Hunger: Wm. Murtha, in memory of his daughter Margaret, age four. Son Peter, daughters Fanny, Catherine, and Mary, all under the age of ten years. 1849—*An Gorta Mór*, likely the time Cornelius stowed away and escaped with his life.

After a short rest for refreshments, they carried on. Soon they were climbing the stone stairs to St. Kevin's hermitage on the banks of the Upper Lake. Deirdre wondered what bird might accompany them along the path to the cave. Surely, they would not be alone without a winged companion. Would it be the Goldcrest, the Redwing, the Wicklow Warbler? But no, it was an ordinary little House Sparrow—*Gealbhan Binne*, just like on her first visit, leading her up the stairs one step at a time towards the site of St. Kevin's Bed. Providing protection and hope, these little birds were often heard before seen, small but strong, "to take their attention upward, reaching, breathless, toward the sparrow's arching flight," as Deirdre had described in her journal.

They found the stones and the remaining footprint of the tiny cell barely large enough to cradle a man's body for sleep. St. Kevin, born at the Fort of the White Fountain, was named *Coemgen*—his name meaning "beautiful shining birth." There were no pains at birth for his mother, so the story was told.

Éamon asked Deirdre to tell him the story of St. Kevin and the blackbird again. She had shared many of the myths and miracles attributed to the saint, but the blackbird was by far the most powerful one and a testament to the saint's ability to transcend the body, even while still walking the earth:

> *And then there was St. Kevin and the blackbird.*
> *The saint is kneeling, arms stretched out, inside*
> *His cell, but the cell is narrow, so*
>
> *One turned-up palm is out the window, stiff*

53

As a crossbeam, when a blackbird lands
And lays in it and settled down to nest.[18]

"Go on Miss Dee, what happened next?"

St. Kevin remained there a fortnight, holding the pose, his quiet position and one outstretched arm remained until the egg was hatched while he stood in solemn prayer. Did he still feel fingers, knees, and toes? Did his body transform to light for those hours and days? Strange miracles always surrounded St. Kevin's world while he walked the earthly sphere. He saved many animals: birds and cows, sheep, and even King O'Toole's pet goose. His love for animals was legendary. Many tales are told or sung in verse.

Alone and mirrored clear in love's deep river,
'To labour and not to seek reward,' he prays.[19]

Éamon and Deirdre stood for a while in that holy place, in a state of wonder and stillness new to them, with Éamon fixing his gaze long enough to feel a deep calm settle in his bones, believing he too could hold his arm outstretched long enough for a blackbird to hatch.

"*Has the shut-eyed blank of underearth / Crept up through him?*"[20] the poem asked.

Deirdre's gaze followed into the misty hollow, a child's memory of her before-the-fire self, a longing for surrender that required no answers or questions. It was here on the banks of the Upper Lake at Glendalough where she heard faint music, the golden timbre of a harp, with graceful notes falling away from strings and soundboard like water moving gently across stones.

*

It was after four when they returned to their lodgings. Hungry, quiet, lost in the day's unfolding, they went to their rooms to rest before supper which was served to guests of the house at six o'clock sharp. Deirdre had set her head down for what she thought would be a tiny nap and woke just in time before the dining bell rang. The only detail of her dream she recalled was the vision of a headstone, marked "1845–1848: *Go ndēana Dia trēcaire ar an-anamacha—* May God have mercy on many souls."

After supper, Deirdre promised to coach Éamon through his repertoire for the festival committee recital. They were both tired from their day, particularly from their time at St. Kevin's Bed, but spirits were high in the great room and other guests had gotten word of the plans for their mini concert. The stage was set by the stone hearth, and fiddles were poised and ready. Éamon had selected as his finale, a rebel song called "*Oró, Sé Do Bheatha 'Bhaile.*" They played together in spirited style this well-known and welcome folk song, the new verses written by nationalist poet Patrick Pearse and often sung by members of the Irish Volunteers during the Easter Rising, and later as a fast march during the Irish War of Independence. This would certainly rouse the guests at their tables!

Deirdre hoped someone would sing along a verse or two and the chorus to accompany their fiddles:

> *Gráinne O'Malley comes over the sea,*
> *With armed warriors as her guard*
> *They're Irishmen—not French nor Spanish*
> *And they will rout the foreigners!*
> *Oh-ro You are welcome home,*
> *Oh-ro You are welcome home,*
> *Oh-ro You are welcome home,*
> *Now that summer's coming!*[21]

Cashel Rock and Little Nellie

THEY DEPARTED GLENDALOUGH EARLY in the morning, taking the M8 motorway to Cork City, then over to Cobh where they had booked lodgings for the festival weekend. The day was not in a hurry and so they had time to make stops and enjoy the country-side. Deirdre always factored in plenty of time when planning a trip, allowing for the unexpected.

Éamon was still asking questions about St. Kevin and the Round Tower well into the first leg of their trip. He was fascinated and at the same time puzzled, having never visited such ancient sites. Although he spent compulsory Sunday mornings at Saint-Jean-Baptiste Catholic Church in Montreal with his foster parents, he had never thought about ruins and graves before. Most of the time at church he was flipping through the missals and hymnals, trying to imagine the music played with a fiddle.

"Why did St. Kevin live alone in that tiny broken stone pit? What did he do all day?" Then Éamon asked, "How did the monks make their ladders tall enough to reach the top of the Round Tower?"

Deirdre couldn't resist quoting Rabindranth Tagore when trying to explain St. Kevin's lifestyle and devotion: "Faith is the bird that feels the light when the dawn is still dark."[22] She also knew that St. Kevin had been led to his partially man-made cave by an angel and his dream was to find god in solitude and prayer. He lived as a hermit for seven years, wearing only animal skins, sleeping on stones, and eating sparingly. "To one who has faith, no explanation is necessary"; so said Thomas Aquinas, and "to one without faith, no explanation is possible." These were not concepts that came easily to Éamon. His thoughts were immersed in music. His faith in family went missing when his mother disappeared, and he hardly remembered her now. She was a vague and distant image, even in photographs. When he had been taken from her, she was at her worst on the streets of Montreal, hardened by poverty and drugs, unable to provide for him even the most rudimentary care. Everything slipped away from his memory, but his new foster folks made up for any sadness with their gifts of kindness and affection. They could not have children of their own, so Deirdre discovered when she finally met Lena and Tomasz Nowak after one of Éamon's school concerts and had the opportunity to hear their stories. She could see that they wore love and kindness on their sleeves and in their deep sad eyes. Éamon was a lucky boy to be welcomed into the Nowak family and given this chance to follow his dreams.

"Sometimes solitude opens invisible doors to silent worlds beyond what our eyes can see," Deirdre added, thinking of St. Kevin and also what Grannie Moll had described of her childhood, spending much time in nature, listening for birds. "The veil is thin, the departed are never far, and solitude is the only road on which to find them," Moll would say.

At the halfway point to Cork, they saw the signs for Cashel and decided they would take their midday break and visit this ancient royal site of the pagan chiefs of Munster. It was a circular stone fort and in St. Patrick's time, it claimed supremacy over all other royal castles—duns, as they were known. Set dramatically above a fertile plain called the Golden Vale, the ancient site was also known as Cashel of the Kings, or St. Patrick's Rock.

Éamon's face lit up when they pulled up in the visitor's parking and he saw the Round Tower. Maybe this time he could climb up into it. Like the tower at Glendalough, the round-headed doorway was just over three meters above ground level and impossible to climb without a rope ladder or a bridge from the cathedral. Built in 1100, the tower was still in good repair. It had four angled windows in the belfry which were slightly set off from the four cardinal points, and there were three linteled windows in the drum.

"These towers are built using the dry-stone method," Deirdre explained, "which is a skilled technique where they did not use mortar to bind them together but used carefully selected interlocking stones. Imagine the perfection and time it would take."

Éamon was still asking questions about solitude and faith while they settled in with their picnic lunch. He wondered if bravery played a part in the puzzle. These kings and saints must have been very brave with all the wounds and suffering in battles. He pictured great kings on dark giant steeds, wearing armor and wielding heavy swords. Éamon was an avid player of Dungeons and Dragons, occasionally participating as the Dungeon Master. He had saved up for months to buy his own sixty-six pack, the "Deck of Many Things."

They took a slow walk through the walled ruin site, first visiting the Hall of the Vicar's Choral, built to house minor clerics who sang during services. Much restoration work was done to make it completely rainproof. It now housed a museum. Next was Cormac's Chapel, a Romanesque-style structure built of sandstone. The five-story Tower House, beside the great Celtic Gothic-style cathedral, was built as a residence for the archbishop.

Deirdre was most interested in Scully's Cross, a gigantic Celtic high cross standing twenty-five feet and visible from the valley below. It sat up on a mausoleum and was made of very fine craftwork with figure sculpture and interlace, a decorative style prevalent in early medieval art. In 1976 the top of the cross was struck by lightning and fell to the ground, one hundred years exactly from the time of the lightning strike on Glendalough's Round Tower. Deirdre took a deep breath and gave Éamon a telepathic glance, knowing he had already read her mind.

After tea and snacks, Deirdre decided it was time to share more with Éamon on the question of faith and to recount the miraculous story of Little Nelly of Holy God, the unofficial patron saint of Cork, who at the age of four-and-a-half was certainly the bravest and most gifted child in the realm of faith and courage, with extraordinary spiritual awareness beyond her tender years.

Éamon settled in on his bench, looking out toward the valley below and feeling a slight breeze across his face. He was comfortable here and felt quite at home. He knew that Deirdre's story, like so many she shared with him in Ireland, would raise more questions but at the same time they always revealed deeper layers of mystery and meaning.

Little Nellie was born in Waterford in 1903. Her original name was Ellen Organ. Her mother had died of tuberculosis when she was just three years old. Her father, a British soldier stationed in Ireland, was no longer able to look after the family after he was posted to Spike Island—once a military fortress and a notorious prison situated just off the shores of Cobh in Cork Harbour.

"Spike Island," Éamon interrupted, recalling the name from his map of Cork City and Cobh. "Can we visit there? I love islands."

Nellie and her sister Mary were sent to the Sisters of Good Shepherd at Sunday's Well in Cork City. This was one of the infamous Magdalene Laundries run by the Catholic Church and supported by the state; an asylum for "fallen women," but also used to house orphans, abused children, and those deserted by their families. So many reports have since surfaced, telling of these asylums and their monstrous practices. So many unmarked graves of women, children, and infants have now been discovered. The Good Shepherd Laundry operated until 1977. The names of at least 195 women and girls who died there have been recorded, but there are large gaps, including the decades between 1896 and 1928, where no records exist. Films and songs about the Magdalene Laundries have become popular in recent years. Deirdre listened to Joni Mitchell's song "Magdalene Laundries" on her album *Turbulent Indigo* when it was first released and had seen Peter Mullan's film *The Magdalene Sisters*.

Deirdre had expected the worst for Little Nellie, but her research told her that the little girl had been treated kindly by the nuns. She lived only eight months at the Sisters of Good Shepherd while she suffered from unrelenting pain and poor health. The list of her afflictions included advanced tuberculosis, whooping cough, a twisted spine, and what was known then as "caries"—a rotting disease of the gums and jaws, with unimaginable pain and the inability to eat food.

Éamon winced, picturing just how terrible the pain would have been, remembering a tooth abscess he had not long ago.

Little Nellie experienced visions and always asked to hear about holy angels. Her mystical life and devotion were limitless, and she was always longing to go to Holy God. Mother Frances described the presence of the great light shining in her heart, the child lost in wonder. Nellie was permitted holy communion at age four years and three months, most unusual and never before permitted by the Vatican. Her feet were so small, the nuns found soft white slippers and socks for her to wear instead of shoes which were the requirement for her first holy communion.

She was in constant pain, but her fortitude and intense prayers transcended her suffering. Her wounds were unspeakable, yet her heart always sang. At the time of her death, she appeared to see something at the foot of her bed, following it overhead with her eyes until she died. She was not yet five years old.

Nineteen months after her death, the Good Shepherd nuns persuaded the authorities to have her body moved from St. Joseph's Cemetery, Turner's Cross in Cork City, to their property at Sunday's Well. When her body was then exhumed, they discovered it was uncorrupted. She appeared exactly the same as when she had been buried. Her limbs were flexible, and her dress and communion veil were like new. The Child of Prague statue was then placed on her grave and the stone inscribed with words from Matthew 19:14, "Suffer little children, and forbid them not, to come unto me: for of such is the kingdom of heaven."[23]

Éamon listened intently to every word that Deirdre spoke. They sat then for a long while, dazed, both lost in a private place of contemplation, imagining Little Nellie.

"We are told that love conquers all things," Deirdre spoke, "and Little Nellie's expression of love through her faith allowed her to withstand the unrelenting pain of her infirmities."

"But was Nellie's god the same as St. Kevin's?" Éamon asked.

*

The drive from Cashel to Cork City and farther to Cobh was a quick easy stretch along the M8. From the Dunkettle Interchange, they followed the signs for Cobh, situated on an island, just twenty minutes farther and over the stunning Belvelly Bridge. They arrived at the Water's Edge Inn along Lower Street and this would be their comfy quarters while they attended the festival in Cork City over the weekend. After checking in and settling their things in their rooms, Deirdre was determined to dangle her feet in the Celtic Sea at last and dunk her special stones which she brought along in a purple and gold Crown Royal whiskey pouch, a remnant from her gigging days in Montreal pubs.

There was a ferry slip from the Kennedy Pier to Spike Island. They talked about visiting the House of Little Nellie on the island where her bedroom remained intact. The *Titanic* memorial was also at the head of the pier, a popular visitors attraction. Cobh was the *Titanic*'s last port of call before it set off on its fatal voyage across the Atlantic. Cobh was often described as the saddest place in Ireland due to the mass exodus of families who embarked at the harbor in the coffin ships, having barely survived the famine. Deirdre sensed the weight of sorrow embedded in the shores of Cobh and hoped she would sleep without night terrors.

Deirdre's prayer that night before bed was a stark reminder:

> *You must grow strong enough to love the world, yet empty enough to sit down at the same table with its worst horrors . . . only in paradox, truth; only in darkness, light.*[24]

Spike Island—Dark Cells and Periwinkles

DEIRDRE AND ÉAMON WOKE early with morning light shining through the gabled windows of their eastside suite. It was their day to scout out the festival venues and get Éamon registered for his recital which was set for Saturday afternoon at the University College Cork's Department of Music, *Roinn an Cheoill.* Deirdre knew the department's reputation to be a center of excellence for both the study and practice of music, with an emphasis on the interdisciplinary and cross-cultural understanding of music. Her fingers and toes were crossed with daily blessings for Éamon, most hopeful that he would dazzle the committee with his performance and be awarded the scholarship to attend the college once he graduated from high school. She believed in his musical talent implicitly and knew he was a very gifted young musician and fiddler, some might describe as a one-of-a-kind musical genius beyond his years and experience, and a pupil she had never encountered before at St. Anne's. When he played, he was transported to another world, another century it seemed, as was the audience. Deirdre knew he had mysteriously inherited the distinct style and ornamentations of an Irish Traveller, something that was inexplicable but nevertheless a large part of his natural ease and passion for the music.

A few of the festival venues were right in Cobh, including Kelly's Bar where Deirdre had performed with her bandmates while in Ireland those years ago.

"Let's go to the sessions at Kelly's tonight," Éamon pleaded, eager to hear what others were playing in Cobh and to join the sessions if possible. Deirdre agreed with some trepidation as she wasn't sure what painful memories might be stirred up at the popular town pub.

First, they would set off on their afternoon junket to Spike Island, just a fifteen-minute ferry ride from Kennedy Pier. On the island they would visit the cottage where Little Nellie had lived and walk the shoreline to beachcomb for shells, just as she must have done before she was handed over to the Good Shepherd Laundry. The cottage was arranged so that visitors to Spike Island could view Little Nellie's bedroom which had been recreated with various holy relics and oddities from the short time she lived there. Their ferry left at half past twelve, so they had just enough time to have a light lunch before heading over to the pier.

Deirdre knew some of the darkest stories about Spike Island's prison, notorious for its "hell on earth," housing thousands of prisoners at various times when it was never designed for such numbers. It had been especially crowded during *An Gorta Mór* when anyone could be thrown in prison for stealing so much as a loaf of bread. There was no distinction between age groups and children were incarcerated. The so-called crime of grand larceny was defined as the theft of any property valued over one shilling, punishable by transportation, which meant deportation out of the country. Spike Island had been intended as a holding station prior to deportation but many inmates never left. It was hard to believe that three thousand years ago, the god-forsaken island began as an early Christian monastery, founded by St. Mochuda.

Along with the Dark Cells, which left prisoners with no light exposure at all, The Punishment Block had been for the penal class, akin to the solitary confinement wings in modern prisons. Here, the prisoners would go mad or commit suicide.

The original star-shaped military fort was built in the late eighteenth century, complete with bastions, ramparts, and a moat—a bleak stone fortress in sharp contrast to the colorful streets and Victorian houses of Cobh which could be seen just a short distance away by water at the head of Cork Harbour.

A bioarchaeologist from the university in Cork, Barra O'Donnabhain, began his extensive research to uncover the dark truths about the draconian history of the Spike Island convict prison, once the largest in the world. O'Donnabhain uncovered many graves and unusual facts about the buried prisoners. Small carved stone artifacts were discovered beneath two cellblocks, bearing primitive designs, one looking like a domino with floral accents on either end. It was the prisoners, of course, who were tasked with the burials of inmates and to build the coffins. It was not surprising that O'Donnabhain found the coffins were built to look respectable, revealing a coat of dark paint to make them appear more dignified than the usual pine boxes. Showing respect for one's fellow inmates despite their tortuous circumstances was a virtue of these Irish inmates.

Deirdre was feeling queasy when they boarded the ferry, knowing that she was about to witness the stone structures and walls and feel the very ground that held the mass suffering and blood of prisoners, many in their teens or younger, and many who had only pinched a loaf of bread to quell their hunger during the famine. She was determined to pay tribute to Little Nellie but knew the island visit would reveal much more. She would feel it in her own veins.

The island seemed small and barren and although it measured one hundred four acres, it was devoid of trees, with only a few low flowering shrubs and hedgerows. The cottage that housed military personnel was where they would find Little Nellie's bedroom. It was sparse, painted in robin's-egg blue, with crisp white linens on a hospital-style cot. On the top sheet was propped a framed photograph showing Nellie in her First Communion dress and veils. It looked like the description of her after she had been exhumed, with clothing and expression intact, body uncorrupted. There was a large crucifix on the windowsill along with two brass candle holders and a mini replica of the Child of Prague statue. At the foot of the bed was a vintage ceramic foot warmer.

There were a few other visitors in the room along with Éamon and Deirdre. No one said a word. A few genuflected and one young woman got down on her knees to pray. Éamon grew pale and wobbly. Deirdre led the way out quickly to get some sea air so that he could breathe freely again. They took the footpath down to the water's edge and had time to bathe their feet in the cool salty water and look for shells. There they found a few cockle shells, heart-shaped with white-and-tan ribbed surfaces. Blue oval-shaped mussel shells were plentiful along with a few dog whelks and periwinkles. Deirdre would take one of each for her gem pouch.

"At least it wasn't the room where she died," Éamon stammered, tripping on his own words.

Deirdre had no intention of visiting the derelict site of the Good Shepherd Laundry which had burned down by suspected arson not that many years ago. Little Nellie's courage, her gift of transcendence from bodily pain and suffering at the hands of fate's cruelty, would stay with them both for some time.

The Parting Glass at Kelly's Bar

COBH'S OWN MUSICIAN, FREDDIE White, was top billing for the festival opening at Kelly's in Casement Square, Ballyvoloon, that night. Éamon couldn't hide his excitement to hear Freddie's masterful guitar techniques and soulful vocals. Maybe he would even have the opportunity and thrill to chat with him after the sessions.

Freddie's musical journey began at the age of thirteen when he played in school bands and later, at seventeen, played professionally. At nineteen he had moved to London, busking in subways where he developed his unique voice and guitar style. How inspiring his story was for Éamon, who knew his life would likely take him on the road with his fiddle, maybe playing in a band in London himself. Freddie was certainly Éamon's musical hero. He would be over the Celtic moon and back that night to have a chance to share a few musical yarns and tips with Freddie. Better yet, Éamon had set his sights on sitting in on the sessions later in the evening after the features while the crowd spilled out onto the front patio chairs. Éamon convinced Deirdre to bring her fiddle down to Kelly's too so they could both sit in. Éamon was not shy when it came to his musical ambitions, and he was convinced that Freddie would be generous in sharing his wisdom. Éamon hoped he would perform a few tunes from his early album *My Country*, the lyrics written by his brother-in-law, the Irish poet Don O'Sullivan, and wouldn't it be brilliant to hear Freddie's rendition of "The Parting Glass" to end his set. Freddie's highly charged and mournful version often inspired tears, with lyrics so close to Celtic sensibilities.

Deirdre was having trouble shaking off Spike Island and the eerie sense of being followed by her ancestors, perhaps great-great uncles who barely survived the famine and then for a morsel of bread pinched from a townsman's table, landed up at the devil's dock on the island and ushered into a windowless cell, never to see the light of day or their family again. There were no signs of Nellie's faith in those dank hallways, no shaking off the chains or black masks to see the light of someone else's god, not that such a ray of light was even possible after all the beatings and starvation. Deirdre could not get the ghostly sounds of their near-silent cries out of her ears, imagining those hollow sunken eyes staring out through a tattered black veil.

"OK, OK, we'll go then, Éamon, just let me get fixed up and ready." Deirdre reluctantly agreed to an evening at Kelly's. Off they went then down Lower Road towards Casement Square, across from the ferry pier. They were welcomed in at the pub like they belonged to the place, a very Cork welcome indeed. They were issued festival tags on lanyards so they could attend all the events over the weekend. With Éamon's recital on the list of young musicians performing for the festival committee, they were both welcome to attend any of the venues in Cobh and Cork City. Their fiddle cases were an obvious sign they were keen to sit in on the sessions. In no time they were invited to join a large table with other guests and offered menus along with a pint of Murphy's.

Freddie was introduced to the standing-room-only crowd at Kelly's by eight p.m. He performed solo with his resonate Gibson and deep baritone voice. His presence filled the room with no need for accompaniment. His dexterity and guitar technique were flawless, and his voice, rising and falling, set the varied moods of the lyrics, everything from tender love songs to words of defiance and battle. It all seemed so natural and effortless. His kind blue eyes and casual turquoise shirt made Éamon feel at ease, like he was part of the extended family of music and song. Freddie finished up his set with "Bad News" from his *Accidental Album* and then, after cheers and shouts, agreed to play "The Parting Glass." It couldn't get better than that, Éamon thought, with Deirdre looking all wispy-eyed and longingly into the distance.

After more rounds of Murphy's, the session musicians took their seats near the stage and started tuning up. Melanie, the woman sitting at their table, invited them to join in, so they took their seats up close and began to tune their fiddles. There were no notions imposed, as was the tradition for these pub sessions. It was all meant to be casual and spontaneous.

Some time into the session, Éamon took the lead, playing his fiddle like he was the chosen lad born in Cobh himself. Others held back during his solo to listen intently. He was a master of the Irish jig, with bright warm sounds and fast tempo. His style was characterized by traditional ornamentations—bowed triplets, fingered rolls, cuts, and long rolls. The sounds flowed through his agile fingers and into the room like a lucid dream. He could tell you everything you needed to know about the nuances of the tunes. His ear recognized each and every variation. Deirdre beamed a huge smile towards Éamon as he finished his solo when the rest of the players joined in with a brilliant finale.

Éamon's talent didn't go unnoticed. It was lucky for him that Freddie had hung around to have a pint or two and socialize with the others. They had their chance finally to meet, a dream of a dream's luck for Éamon.

Deirdre was up at the bar to cover their tab and thought they should get away early since Éamon had his recital the next day. This was when she spotted a head of jet-black curly hair striding in the door with a fiddle case. The face was unmistakable. It was Rory—*Ruairí* Callaghan—the young and talented heartbreaker that she had met when playing sessions in Kinsale on her first trip. Would he recognize her now? Could she bear to see him like this after such a sorrowful parting, such long-lasting grief that she struggled with back home, knowing they could never have made it work?

"Deirdre, it that you?" Rory asked, stepping right up to the bar boldly like it had only been yesterday since they last met.

Of course, she was lost for words and didn't say a thing before he took her in his arms and gave her the biggest squeeze, followed by that distinctive quality of a Rory Callaghan kiss. Oh my, she thought, we can't possibly start this up again. It will take me another four years to recover.

They sat drinking a pint together and caught up on their news, as much as could be shared about what felt like a century since they last had locked eyes and arms. He had seen her off at the train station when she parted Kinsale to return to Canada. She had turned down any invitation to remain in Ireland as she would never abandon her commitment with Trifinity at St. Anne's. The truth be told, her heart was frightened and had remained closed tight since the fire of her childhood, despite her forays into the dating world, one mistake at a time. No man had so much as pried the bolt lock on her history over the years. No man had tempted her as Rory had those months she spent carefree in Kinsale, as if her former self, stunted by flame and sorrow, was put to rest so she could fly with the Sparrowhawk that circled most evenings, heralding inner strength hidden there all the while. The small yet fierce bird of prey brought unexpected resilience, a messenger of protection, courage, and clear sight.

Rory offered to walk them back to their inn. Éamon was still jubilant that he had met Freddie and encouraged by him to follow his path faithfully with his music. Freddie was positive Éamon would excel at his recital and, not far into the future, would be back in Cork at the university on a scholarship.

They reached Water's Edge Inn and after Éamon was settled in his room, Deirdre joined Rory back at the lobby so they could take their waterfront walk, a promise they made at the pub before leaving.

How could they possibly describe the years that had passed since they parted? The fire that was kindled that summer in Kinsale was never extinguished. Their alchemy did not need words or explanation. They walked to the pier. The kiss that would not end became an invisible bond. The kiss went on as they stood under the light of June's pre-solstice moon on the pier, leaving her lips with a bright crimson glow from his hunger's urgency. His essence had not vanished during those cold lonely winters in Montreal. What was she to do now under such an indelible spell?

The hours passed as they sat on a bench near the water's lip. Rory held on to her with both arms around her shoulders, her windswept curls and pale cheeks pressed against his chest. The sweet scent of agapanthus and spicy hyacinth was captured in the evening breeze and rose up from flower beds on the strand. This is what she would remember when morning light arrived. This was the scent that would conjure the kiss a continent away.

"We can't be sitting on this bench all night, Deirdre," Rory whispered.

They both knew their parting, inevitably, would be filled with confusion and anticipatory grief of the living kind, once again, as it had been those years ago, even more sorrowful now this time around, knowing the flame had not been extinguished, not even by a flicker's second.

> For the test of the heart is trouble, and it always comes
> with years. And the smile that is worth the praises of earth,
> is the smile that shines through the tears.[25]

Éamon's Recital—*Port na bPúcaí*

ÉAMON WOKE EARLY, KNOWING it was going to be a grueling day, one that would require every ounce of his best musical performance and abilities. For extra luck he had his special fiddle for this occasion. He had managed to purchase the McNella finally at the end of term with hard-earned paper route money. He spent several hours rehearsing and going over his tablature, which was hardly necessary but gave him a sense of order and focus. His ability to memorize music composition after only hearing it once was commended by his first teachers and this playing-by-ear gift followed him straight through school to the Trifinity classes. He remembered one grouchy teacher in grade school accusing him of cheating since he couldn't transcribe the musical notations on staff paper after playing. But it was all by ear, he knew. Not cheating. The teacher had not been pleased and gave him a poor grade in music that year.

Deirdre brought him tea to the room along with a healthy breakfast of eggs and a batch of boxty with candied bacon, knowing he would need the extra energy for his recital. Nerves would cause them both to skip the afternoon meal, and they would be leaving for the university campus by midday. They were required to check in by one o'clock to determine what room they were assigned. There were twelve students in the youth category from countries around the world competing for three scholarships that would be awarded the week after the recitals. The students would be asked to play four prepared pieces of their own choice, which had been thoroughly rehearsed back at home. The final test was to play a piece picked by the committee. Éamon would not find out the jury's choice until the time of his finale performance. They would provide him with the title and sheet music and he would be expected to play it flawlessly.

Éamon dressed in his best outfit, a white shirt and tie with navy corduroy pants. His hair would be tamed as best could be, but Deirdre thought his wild curls made a fine statement of their own.

Off they went, back across the Belvelly Bridge to Cork City and on to the grounds to Cork College University situated centrally, not far from the River Lee.

The recital hall was in the main Music Department building. They arrived at the arched double doors, painted sky blue with heavy iron hinges. On the wall next to the door was a plaque stating it was the building's 135th birthday. Then Éamon saw the sign that read "136 Sunday's Well, Cork College Department of Music." He shot a glance at Deirdre as they went through the doors, whispering, "Sunday's Well! Is this the building where Little Nellie died?"

Both were relieved to learn from the custodian who had greeted them that the Good Shepherd Convent—the Magdalene Laundry—once a red-brick and stately building as well, was located further along Sunday's Well Road but had burned down by an unknown arsonist in 2008 and was now derelict. They both sighed in relief.

Éamon was nervous but confident and figured Deirdre was showing her nerves more than he was feeling. So much weighed on these fleeting moments of his recital, their shared musical life culminating in this very place and time. If Éamon won the scholarship, he would have a once-in-a-lifetime chance to attend the most musically diverse program in all of Ireland. He could then go on to graduate studies, the MA program that specialized in traditional Irish music. Deirdre had no doubt he would make the grades and succeed with an international career in the future. It was not just his technical skills and interpretation of the music but his whole body spoke the language. If music moves through the body like a dancer moves weightless through air, Éamon was a master of both. His body, all lean muscles and limbs, even his wild auburn hair, moved in unison with the notes, the rhythm, the emotion dancing through his hands and fiddle bow, his passion expressed in his facial features.

By the time his recital schedule was posted, they had exactly half an hour to cool their nerves, saying a prayer together for *Ceridwen* and *Taliesin*, Celtic goddess and god of music, poetry, magic, and wisdom, to prepare their hearts and minds for this challenge. Deirdre promised to hold him in her gaze while he played, knowing that he would be fully absorbed by the music but would feel her support beaming through the throng of bodies in the audience. He could see her clearly from his position on the stage and the energy between them was empathic. Together, they had created this day.

*

Éamon rose beyond all expectations and was fully transported to the core of his musical gift. His face, so fine and innocent, wore the expression of a passionate troubadour who played for pure inspiration and joy. The energy was palpable in the room. Not a sound came from the guests or committee members while Éamon's signature ornamentations moved instinctively through the room. Like the flow of a full autumn river, the mood was abundant with the cycles of life. The sounds were uniquely his own. The time then came for Éamon to perform his finale, the committee's choice, a slow air—"*Port na bPúcaí*."

Holy Jaysus, Deirdre whispered. The very piece he had studied and practiced so diligently but decided at the last minute not to include in his repertoire for the recital. It was the mournful air that he loved and played like an angel. It was a long piece, the title translated as "The Song of the Faeries," and ran just under five minutes. Every second would count to the committee judges. His execution was flawless. He was able to create the cries and wails with the fiddle, leaving the room in awe and bringing tears to many listeners in the room. No doubt this slow air was chosen not because of its subtle complexities but purely for its intensity of emotion and how it would evoke Éamon's pure musical response.

When Éamon finished, he stood up, bowed, and appeared to glow under the light that shone from the stained-glass windows above, just as he took those few moments to regain his orientation back to the world and the room. Maybe he was beamed to the very beaches of Great Blasket Island where the song was conceived, hearing those voices of the spirits and the whales that circled off the Dingle Peninsula.

Poets and Nationalists, Clonakilty

DEIRDRE AND ÉAMON WERE bone-tired after their epic day at the recital. They returned to Cobh following a short reception with various event officials and other musicians. Formalities were not their strong point. Arrangements were made to contact the college in five days' time to learn the results of the competition, just before they were to catch their flight home to Montreal.

As they drove away from the music building, they saw in the distance across campus the fires from the Bonna Night celebrations and considered for a moment whether they should join the pagan festivities. Much singing, dancing, blessings, and merriment would continue throughout the night, but they were too weary from the day's demands and excitement and now hungry for a meal. They thought best not to stretch their energies but rather to jump through the imaginary fires of Bonna Night in their dreams, saying blessings to the goddess Áine for a long warm summer.

Their last night in Cobh included a walk on the town promenade and then a hearty supper of seafood chowder and heavily buttered soda bread at their inn's eatery, Jacob's Ladder, a fitting name reminding Deirdre of the story of Jacob's dream. What stood out from her long-ago and tedious studies in catechism was the divine connection between heaven and earth—often a ladder—a wishful prayer in her own dreams of family, especially after the house fire. A divine ladder could have saved them all. Protection, exclaimed the nuns, speaking of Jacob's ladder during their lessons—exactly what Deirdre and Éamon needed as they journeyed further into West Cork, on to Clonakilty, the Drombeg Circle, and then to Skibbereen to uncover the story of Deirdre's ancestors and maybe even Great-Grandfather Cornelius, who survived *An Gorta Mór* without so much as a portion of bread, and certainly no ladder.

Éamon figured they should each place a stone under their pillow that night, just like Jacob under the stars, remembering the lessons at parochial school. He imagined the stone might bring them light and luck through their dreams. Then he asked Deirdre if they would be visiting Drombeg's Circle on their way to Skibbereen. After having his vivid dream that night at home, he found pictures and diagrams of the stone circle in the visitor's pamphlet and wanted to sit at The Druid's Altar himself.

The very name "Clonakilty" in Irish meant "stone castle of the woods," sometimes shortened to "Clon" for stone. The standing stones at Drombeg, all local sandstone, were from the middle or later period of the Bronze Age, about three thousand years ago.

Deirdre slept fitfully that night, her last at the Water's Edge Inn, waking often and certain she heard the sounds of the coffin ships alongside at the Port of Cobh, maybe even the barque Lady Kennaway departing with the orphan girls from the Cork Workhouse, sounding the ship's horn in a long loud blast as the ship pulled away.

*

The afternoon drive to Clonakilty from Cobh was just over an hour and once they settled in at their booked lodgings, the Old Stables Studio Cottage, they planned an early evening at DeBarra's Folk Club, legendary for its over-the-top music lineup, even acknowledged as a must-visit venue in The Lonely Planet. They would then drive a little farther to Drombeg's Circle in time for the solstice sunset.

As an axial stone circle, the megalithic site contains two taller entrance stones placed opposite the altar's recumbent stone. During the summer solstice, the setting sun aligned with the sacred well. They would sit next to the recumbent stone, The Druid's Altar, watching the sky turn from rose to indigo, and listen for messages from the Druids.

"Éamon, did you know who was the most famous person that lived in Clonakilty?" She knew he would not be up on all the rebel politics of Ireland but was sure he remembered the name of Michael Collins from their long-animated chats about Irish history as they prepared for their journey. Collins, director of intelligence for the Irish Republican Army during the Irish War of Independence, attended the local boys' national school in Clonakilty. He gave several orations from O'Donovan's Hotel on Main Street and a statue and museum were set up in the town in his honor. He may have visited DeBarra's as a young lad, over a hundred years ago, looking for a loaf of bread when the pub was then a typical grocery bar with a bakery and storehouse to the rear.

"They had a price on his head, £10,000. He was assassinated here in Cork at the age of thirty-one. Shot to death. Fighting for Irish Independence. A Nationalist hero right to his grave."

Deirdre was also keen to share more with Éamon about Ireland's fiercely fought road to independence. Mary Jane O'Donovan Rossa, another Clonakilty activist who became a published poet of note, was born just as the famine began and died in 1916. Her father had been a member of the Young Ireland movement, a political and cultural group committed to the fight for independence. Mary Jane came by her activism naturally. Her husband, Jeremiah O'Donovan Rossa, was an Irish Fenian leader who was one of the key members of the Irish Republican Brotherhood, the IRB. Mary Jane's brothers also signed up for the IRB. She eventually fled to America and was followed later by her husband once he was released early from his twenty-year jail sentence with the condition to leave the country. They both published books in America. They died a year apart in New York and their bodies were brought back to Ireland for burial, interred in Glasnevin Cemetery, Dublin.

Deirdre read a few lines to Éamon from Mary Jane's poem, "A Voice for Ireland," speaking out for unity: "*Up, men of the West! Are you sleeping or dead? / Do you hear not the wall of the anguish you bred? / For the blood that is shed on the scaffold's dull height / Is yours to avenge if you boldly unite."*[26]

Then Deirdre closed with lines from Mary Jane's "Song of Freedom":

> *The long night flies; see in freedom's skies*
> *Fierce lights are breaking!*
> *And the torpid land from its icy hand*
> *Of misery is waking.*
> *Arise! our exiled brothers call,*
> *Arise! uplift the tearful pall*
> *From Erin.*[27]

The Drombeg Circle

It was getting on for midevening, summer solstice, with lovely pale blue skies and hints of orange and pink, a scattering of wispy cirrus clouds, anticipating the sunset as they drove from Clonakilty to the Drombeg Circle. Deirdre opened her guide map of rural West Cork to make sure she was following the best route. In reliable Irish fashion, the directions were friendly if not meandering: "Take N71 west to Ross Carberry. Just after the causeway take a left turn onto the R597. Then after about four kilometers take another left turn. You will see the sign-post for Drombeg Circle, also written in the Irish Gaelic of course, *Cloch-Cheacal Agus Cairn,* meaning 'the small ridge.' The car park will be on the right about 400 meters further along up the road. Then you'll be there. The site for the Circle is reached via a gravelly path around 150 meters or so, and then you must cross a grassy field that is relatively firm and even. Wet conditions may make the field more difficult."

"Miss Dee, what is a Druid?" Éamon asked as they pulled up to park. "Will we see a Druid in the Circle?"

Deirdre took a while to answer, mostly because there isn't a simple answer to the mysteries of Druidism. They left no written accounts, and their knowledge and traditions were passed down orally from generation to generation. Storytelling and recitation were their means of communication.

"Druids were often thought of as bards, poets, philosophers, holding hidden esoteric knowledge. They believed in the entity of the spirit. They held ceremonies and had a deep connection with Mother Earth."

"Éamon, there are modern-day Druids too. They have formed groups all over the world and call their assemblies 'groves'—Order of Bards, Ovates, Druids. I read about them in *The Irish Times*."

"Will we have a ceremony tonight?" Éamon's voice was eager.

Deirdre had brought her pouch of shells and stones, choosing an agate that she had collected from the eastern shores of Lake Superior to place under the hawthorn tree on the hill next to Drombeg's entrance. A lone hawthorn was the gateway between this world and the next. She also brought her beeswax candle packed specifically for the occasion.

"We can say some blessings for our ancestors, and let's say a prayer, asking if Great-Grandfather Cornelius will send us a message. Once we get to Skibbereen I will find out more about my family from the famine records held at the Heritage Center. I will also meet with my ancestry group. They've set up a special event just for our visit the day after tomorrow."

The landscape near the circle was a patchwork quilt of gradually flowing slopes and rounded hilltops, lined with shrubs of bright yellow gorse and white viburnum lacecaps. The landscape was also lit up with bright flowers of the sacred hawthorn, *Sceach Gheal*, sometimes referred to as the beauty of the faery tree, or whitethorn. Each flower cluster contains five petals, at times color-changing from white to a blushed pink hue. The flowers have a sickly sweet scent, often associated with death. The unpleasant smell attracts carrion insects for pollination, but the flowers with their multiple stamens and reddish anthers also attract bees, and oh, the honey from the Hawthorn! The bushes form a natural hedge with their prickly thorns, helping to contain farmers' livestock. They spotted a few buildings in the distance, with cattle and sheep grazing peacefully, and a glimpse of the sea beyond.

Deirdre and Éamon entered the Drombeg site, taking the path along the low sloping rise of rural land to the circle situated at the head of a long green valley. From there they could see the *Fulacht Fiadh*, a well-preserved prehistoric mound of heat-altered stone, used to heat up and boil water in a trough. It was connected to the circle by a causeway.

Of the seventeen original stones, thirteen remained. In the circle's center was a burial site where the cremated remains of an adolescent were found after the site had been excavated in the mid-1950s. Some legends hold that it was a young chieftain, likely sacrificed by the Druids. The Druid's Altar is situated opposite the two seven-foot entrance stones. It is a darker, recumbent stone which looks very much like a sacrificial altar. The circle is celestial-aligned, marking both the winter and summer solstices with the setting sun.

The light was now getting dimmer, sunset just a half hour away. Deirdre suggested they sit in front of The Druid's Altar to say their blessings. Soon the sun would set over the rise and, perfectly aligned, fall into the well.

Deirdre read from her journal: "Family constellations, show me what kindles between us, not unusual, this knowing field that tempts our embrace / our hearts' chambers now synchronized, ready for the telling."[28]

A little farther along, she read, "Blue light clears a path for you. Ó hAodha, trees of Ogham: whitethorn, pine and yew, the last being crann sailí, the willow tree."[29] She had translated her family name using the Ogham alphabet with its corresponding trees. "History never linear / where we speak only syllables, guttural in the dark."

Éamon's blessing was short, simple: "Lord of the fiddle, bring me back to Cork so I may follow my heart's desire."

"Well done, Éamon. *Blessed be, may it be so.*"

Deirdre lit her beeswax candle and held it up to the moon, now beaming an ominous lunar halo, heralding a storm beyond the cirrus clouds, just days from the Mead Moon.

The ancients believed the moon hung over the central stone and the Celts had an hour to honor the celestial body. It was also believed the circle was aligned to the North Star.

Deirdre and Éamon both became quiet, drifting into deep reverie. Not more than ten minutes passed when Deirdre heard the sweet sounds of a tin whistle off in the distance. She looked up and towards the leading pathway. The sky was painted now a twilight hue, prolonged, timeless. She was not sure she could trust her eyes. The shape of a man appeared to be climbing the rise towards the circle. He was playing his tin whistle beautifully, walking at a leisurely pace with an uneven gait, looking familiar upon the land amongst the stones as though he belonged.

He wore a brown scally cap, simple knee-length leine and leggings, old boots of untanned leather with wooden plattens to keep his feet dry. When he reached the Circle, he greeted them by name.

"Well then you'll be Deirdre I expect," he said with an impish grin. "And the lad, you must be Éamon."

"How did you know our names?" Deirdre asked, bewildered. She could hardly find her voice. He smiled.

"How are you liking the old country my dear, now that you are here again?" he inquired in soft lilting tones with a Cork accent—known for its melodic quality and elongated vowel sounds—smiling once again.

Deirdre and Éamon did not say a word, sharing puzzled glances, not wanting to break the mood set by their unexpected guest. They knew that he had arrived from beyond the veil. Éamon was accustomed to Deirdre's stories and experiences with the unseen world and had several himself when he was preschool age, frequently induced by dreams.

They sat a while, all three, then Deirdre poured hot tea from the thermos she had brought along for their ceremony. They sipped the warm herbs together and waited for the sun's spectacular departure.

"I expect you will be coming to my wake, then," he said in a tone of certainty, breaking the silence. "It will be in two days' time, over in Skibbereen, near Abbeystrowry."

The sun was now fully set beyond the fields and horizon. It grew dark quickly. Deirdre stood to stretch her legs and to say it was time to go. The old man rose, tipped his hat, wandered off through the entrance stones back down the path, and was quickly gone. They heard his tin whistle again, this time playing the closing tune from "Dear Old Skibbereen." Deirdre remembered the lyrics:

Oh Father dear I often hear your speak of Erin's Isle,
Her lofty scenes and valleys green, her mountains rude and wild.
They say it is a lovely land wherein a prince might dwell,
Oh why did you abandon it?[30]

The Weeping Well, *An Gorta Mór*

DEIRDRE AND ÉAMON RETURNED to their cottage lodgings, not sharing a word about the old man they had met at Drombeg Circle. They were both familiar enough with spirit entities. Could it be that they imagined him at the same time? Was he truly of flesh and blood, or a *thevshi*—a spirit caught between this world and the next, or was he ancestral—*spioraid na sinsear*?

Tired beyond words, Éamon took a cup of milky tea up to his bedroom in the loft and settled in quietly for sleep. They would be leaving in the morning for Skibbereen, their last village visit, before returning to Dublin and then home. Sleep was soon on its way, faster than he could finish his tea.

Deirdre fell asleep in her chair while reading a book about Skibbereen and James Mahony, eyewitness to the famine tragedy, who published his account in *The Illustrated London News* after his visit to West Cork in 1847. His descriptions of starvation, the victims of famine, the deplorable and overcrowded conditions of the workhouses, the rampant diseases and slow deaths suffered by so many, were accompanied by his graphic depictions. His sketches were heartrending. Readers of the *London News* had not been prepared for Mahony's shocking articles and depictions of the horrors of famine. Assistance then began to pour in after his article was published. Skibbereen became known as the epicenter of *An Gorta Mór* while livestock was plentiful and readily exported to England; 9992 calves in 1847, with tens of thousands of firkins of butter, nine gallons each, along with salmon, oysters, herring, peas, beans, and onions. In the face of starvation, ships pulled out of Dublin Harbour throughout *An Gorta Mór*, bearing feasts for the gentry.

Deirdre shook herself awake from her nightmarish half-sleep and went to bed. A dream of familiar and wrenching imagery followed her there:

The woman is back at the weeping well, her shawl and blouse in tatters. Her feet are bare but beside the stone base of the well, she finds a pair of battered and muddy brogues.

She reaches into the well for the ladle and bucket hanging on a frayed rope, hearing voices below, calling for help, calling again, pleading for a morsel to ease their hunger. She drops the bucket down into the deep well, sending a small ration of bully beef and bread, all that she had carried in her pack for the day's supper. She hears a mumble of voices echoing up from the stone wall, then a splash as the bucket touches water. She pulls it back up slowly and finds it is now empty of food but sees a tarnished amulet of tin and copper, safely resting in the ladle.

She reads a note left behind at the bedside by the watchman in her dream while she is still dreaming:

> "The Aglish Cross, The Ogham Stone, 6th or 7th century MAQI MAQI . . . GGODIKA—the client of the Descendant of Vu
> The Maltese Cross—an early Church emblem of the Knights of St. John, depicting eight points within the circle—a symbol of the fire service"

Skibbereen and the Famine Story

SKIBBEREEN WAS NOT FAR along the N71 from Clonakilty. Deirdre and Éamon took time for a morning walk near their Stables Cottage before heading off, reflecting on the night and their unexpected visitor, the old man at Drombeg. They decided to name him Connor, *Conchobar* to be sure in Irish, lover of wolves and master of hounds.

"I dreamed of wolves last night," said Éamon. "They were hungry and running all night, looking for small game, the bloodier the better, to be sure."

"There are no wolves in Ireland now," Deirdre said, certain the gray wolves had been extinct after losing their native forest habitat. "Last one found was in the late 1700s. Humans are the enemies, always the real predators of nature's beauty."

"What about your dream, Miss Dee?"

"The old souls in my dream were hungry too but certainly they were not wolves. Voices crying out for food. You will learn more when we reach Skibbereen."

*

They arrived and met with their hosts at the Skibbereen Heritage Center. It had been arranged for them to stay at Annie May's Inn, right in the heart of the town. Terri Kearney and Philip O'Regan, both historians native to Skibbereen, poured their heart and soul into their work, bringing awareness of the tragedy, for so long untold, through their book *Skibbereen, The Famine Story*.[31] The stories were also shared through the Center's exhibit which included some of the well-known sketches by James Mahony. A guided walking tour brought visitors along on a virtual journey of remembrance through the most devastated areas of the town. There were as many paupers in workhouses as people in the village in 1847, confined to their two-foot square space. Many argued that the word "famine" did not convey the truth about what was later called the worst demographic catastrophe of nineteen-century Europe. Ireland had food and plenty, shipped out regularly, but not available to the poor whose staple was the potato, and for five years the blight took away their lifeline. Potatoes and buttermilk were considered a complete diet for the rural poor. They were forced to surrender their grain to pay rent or be evicted. It was an incurable, unholy curse, ending in slow death for well over a million people.

Siobhan Byrne from Deirdre's ancestry group met up with them at the Center in the afternoon. She was anxious to share that a special event was planned the next day which would bring many answers to Deirdre's questions about her Irish family. Siobhan didn't elaborate but told her the event would take place over at a heritage house next to Abbeystrowry.

Siobhan also invited them to attend a dramatized reading planned at the Skibbereen Heritage Center that night. Presentations would be made, telling of the famine years, sharing dark stories, chronicles, songs and music of *An Gorta Mór*. The evening would begin at seven over at Levis's Quay, the original location of Swanton's Store, which became an emergency workhouse and soup kitchen.

"Thank goodness for Terri and Philip who collected some of these stories in their book and now share them with the world. For more than a century the shame, carried by Irish survivors, caused the truth to be buried along with the dead in their shallow graves."

Siobhan was not a fan of foreign academics with their many published volumes and biased views, much like the opinions held of all wars of the world, written in hindsight from comfortable armchairs or university offices, prejudiced according to nationality and who was telling whose war, and whose victory was won.

Deirdre anticipated an intense evening but none of it was new to her. The research tore at her, leaving her raw and beyond the capacity to assimilate such horror. She often found herself in restless sleep, wondering how many of her family members died without so much as a proper burial with coffin and gravestone.

Then she opened Terri and Philip's book to the very page: the message on the memorial stone at Abbeystrowry, exactly as she had dreamed back at Glendalough: "*Go ē ndēana Dia trōcaire ar an-anamacha*"—May God have mercy on many souls.

*

The Levis's Quay was crowded with a large audience for the evening event, a dramatic reading by the Skibbereen players called *God Rest Their Souls*. All the characters were dressed in period costumes. A children's musical quartet was sitting to the left of the makeshift stage with fiddle, tin whistles, and bodhrán poised to play. Lecterns were arranged from which each speaker would deliver their soliloquy.

The printed program was circulated, describing the cast of characters. Deirdre read the playbill which included haunting descriptions of people who survived the famine, or not. The readings began with Dr. Daniel Donovan, a successful surgeon, a writer, and a champion of the destitute, whose name will never be forgotten in Skibbereen. He eventually succumbed to the fever himself. James Mahony, the journalist who traveled to Skibbereen, provided eyewitness accounts of the horrors. His graphic drawings and descriptions were published in *The London Illustrated Times* in his article "Sketches of the West of Ireland." Little Tommy Guerin, who was buried alive in the shallow famine pits of Abbeystrowry and lived to tell the tale, walking with a limp from broken knees. Even the Choctaw Nation chief spoke, telling how his people survived the ruinous Trail of Tears, but heard the plight of the starving Irish in 1847 and took up a collection, sending money to Cork.

Kindred spirits were the Choctaws, in kindness and compassion. More stories were shared.

"Skibbereen is the magnate of misery," shouted a nameless British politician in the cast. "The Irish property owners must solve their own Irish poverty problem!"

Joseph Murphy, who lived on *Inis Uí Drisceoil* (Heir Island) when *The Susan* was wrecked on the rocks just off Reen Point, declared: "It was a godsend for the starving people of the island, scrambling to collect a healthy cargo of wheat. Christmas Eve, 1848."[32] Joseph was promptly shot by the coast guard. Someone offstage to the right let off a small prop pistol to punctuate the sound of Joseph's death. The audience startled.

Each character spoke directly and with finality, staring into the audience with compelling eyes. No one moved or shuffled in their seats. During Tommy Guerin's story, Éamon grabbed Deirdre's hand, his palm cold and sweating.

The program ended with the young musicians playing the town's anthem, "Dear Old Skibbereen." People rose from their chairs in standing ovation with rounds of applause, which somehow seemed unfitting after the harrowing delivery of such grim and true accounts. The audience then broke into the chorus verse from "The Fields of Athenry," the folk ballad considered the unofficial national anthem of both the Irish at home and across the Irish diaspora worldwide:

> *Low lie the fields of Athenry / Where once we watched the small free birds fly / Our love was on the wing / We had dreams and songs to sing / It's so lonely 'round the fields of Athenry.*[33]

PART THREE

The Wake of Cornelius Eoin Ó hAodha

Healing occurs in the manner of Creation: Cell by Cell.
Shimmering, coursing through the molecules, stirring the waters of
life.[34]

—Joyce Whiteley Hawkes, *Cell-Level Healing: The Bridge from Soul to Cell*

The Graves Are Walking

Siobhan arrived early, rapping on the door of Deirdre's room at Annie May's Inn in Bridge Street. She knocked louder a second time, hearing Deirdre inside the door, struggling with the old chain lock. Was it that time already? The breakfast table wasn't even set downstairs for the inn's guests.

Deirdre knew it was going to be an all-out day, likely to reveal new stories and mysteries. She had laid out her only summer dress on the chair the night before, an embroidered mid-length teal shift layered with lace collar and sleeves. She expected that Siobhan's ancestry group had prepared a full day's program of genealogy presentations and long sessions comparing family trees. The history of West Cork, especially in and around Skibbereen during the years of *An Gorta Mór*, would be shared and members of the Heritage Center had been invited to participate. She knew from Siobhan's conversation that new documents had been discovered, and family ties and trees might at last be uncovered.

All the preparations leading up to the day brought back vivid memories for Deirdre of her trip to the Aran Islands and her visit to Ronan's shop, An Púcán, on *Inis Mór* just outside Kilronan. The shop had many curios with knitted scarves and socks made by locals. Deirdre had her eye on a bodhrán, the native drum of the Celts. Ronan was at least a decade older than Deirdre and had that weathered look of an islander in the *Gaeltacht*. She had corresponded with him after seeing his name show up on her DNA ancestry report. She knew it was a long shot and likely would lead nowhere, but feeling the magnetic pull to visit the Aran Islands was part of her search on that first trip to Ireland. She spent days going through files of paperwork and old photographs that Ronan had collected from his grandparents; photographs of what might well be second or third cousins once removed. One picture of a tall man, likely in his late twenties with the scribbled date of 1870 on the back, showed him standing by an open peat fire in a thatched cottage, much like the hearth in Ronan's shop. A second picture showed the handsome man tending to a large kettle hanging from the pot crane, ready to make a strong black tea. The man had a look that sent shivers through her, not from fear or malice but from a deep familiarity, a chemistry that could not be explained. His features looked similar to Grandfather Liam Séamas when he was younger. She had committed many of the photographs from family albums to memory, all lost in the house fire. She had once seen a faded and torn picture that her father kept of Great-Grand-father Cornelius, likely the only picture that existed he said, but Deirdre would never forget his face. She took in a big breath and then sighed when Ronan shook his head, muttering, then spit out the following protest.

"They all look alike don't they. We hope to find our kin one day beyond every picture or grave, but they were all lost to the likes of Cromwell, that zealous plunderer, the devil himself who parceled out all the land. Then the blight arrived on ships. Cottiers at the hands of greed ejected, pushed farther and farther up the hillsides with nothing but sand for soil to plant their potato patches—*lazy gardens* they were called. All meager abodes of mud and thatch set ablaze. Families left to starvation and disease. God rest their souls."

Ronan's rant now stilled by the sparks from his hearth fire, his face flushed at the same time he was holding back tears. He poured himself a whiskey, the bottle gracing the shelf beside the till. All this made Deirdre think of words shared by John Kelly in his book *The Graves Are Walking*, where he declared, "No wonder so many Irish immigrants were incapable of saying 'England' without adding 'Goddamn her.'"

Deirdre shook herself out from the deep lingering memories of her visit to Ronan's shop on Inis Mór on her first journey to Ireland and quickly got ready for the day. Éamon was already dressed and eager to go, anticipating another long day of unsettling stories and much mournful music. He would bring his fiddle just in case.

Siobhan drove them over to Abbeystrowry Cemetery off Schull Road opposite River Ilen which rises at Mullaghmesha Mountain and flows nearly forty kilometers into the Celtic Sea. Deirdre imagined that the River Ilen would provide comfort for all the souls buried in those mass famine pits across the road. Their spirits would travel like the sea trout or the Atlantic salmon back down the river to the afterlife, at last set free.

A little farther along was the heritage house that had been hired for the day's event. It was sparse from the outside, neatly whitewashed with well-kept gardens and a half-wall hedged perimeter and entranceway. The morning sun had finally shown up and blown off the clouds, with June's glory and warm hints of citrus yellow along with subtle golden undertones bathing the skies.

Neither Deirdre nor Éamon knew just what the long day's proceedings would hold. They imagined a sumptuous midday meal with all the trimmings along with presentations on genealogy and local history. Traditional Irish music would be offered between talks, and small groups would then form to pore over family trees. This was much like the ancestry meetings that took place back home in Montreal but ultimately led to dead ends each time. This day would be quite different.

They were greeted at the door by several thin men, appearing like pallbearers, grim and pale, saying "sorry for your trouble" in a low voice over and over to each guest. Perhaps they were groomsmen, and the day would develop into a wedding. Others began to arrive, and the front room quickly became full. Siobhan showed Deirdre their seats in the formal dining hall where tables were arranged, laden with mountains of sandwiches, biscuits, and sweets, along with copious pots of tea and jugs of milk.

They heard a bustling at the door and in walked a small group of women, seven in total, all wearing period costumes including full-length wool skirts, charcoal-tinted and tweed-flecked, along with black shawls draped over their foreheads and hair. The keening women moved quickly through the hall and into the sitting room.

Finally, Siobhan asked for quiet in the room and led everyone in a blessing for the families now gathered, each one hopeful for answers and a peaceful heart at last.

It was clear to Deirdre now that the event was in fact a wake—a *tórramh,* or a communal *faire*—where all attendees would mourn their lost relatives who remained nameless in Abbeystrowry, but now their spirits could depart with the blessings of a wake. There was always a feast at such a gathering, with food prepared by neighbors and kin.

The keening women, *mná chaointe,* began their laments, gathered in the sitting room—a sustaining ritual to soothe fear and contain the sadness, the words of their songs improvised, often poetic with non-lexical utterances. The watchers gathered around what appeared to be a plain pine coffin, held up on a large Victorian oak pedestal table. The *mná chaointe* moved in closer, gathering near to the coffin's side. The corpse was indistinguishable, veiled with whitesmoke netting, the body being a representation of all loved ones who had passed beyond the veil.

Deirdre checked in with Éamon frequently to make sure he was all right with the events as they were unfolding. She knew he was well beyond his years in wisdom, unflappable in most ways, and created his own sense of magic realism through his discoveries of worlds beyond the everyday. She sat beside him now in the great room and reached for his hand to reassure him as they waited for Siobhan to begin what she thought would be a eulogy.

The keening continued, a cathartic venting of grief meant to drain away the well of tears in the room. How long would this last, Éamon wondered? Deirdre knew that traditional wakes were a grand social and community event that journeyed through at least one solar cycle—day, night, and then day. During these hours of mingling darkness, a portal would open between the living and mystical worlds, allowing the souls of the deceased to depart in peace. The dead needed the intervention of the living through prayers, abundant nourishment, blessings, and lively music to ease them into the next realm. Wake-goers would often lean in and kiss the corpse, making death a tangible fact and not something to be feared. Children would ruffle the hair of the deceased and were encouraged to reach out to them, touching their arms or hands. Laughter was the guest of honor.

"Why have we lost our way with death?" Deirdre whispered to herself, where hushed silence was the expected response and the corpse whisked away, never to be seen. No one at home ever spoke of it. The fragments that Deirdre recalled of her family's funeral service were hushed in silence and remained behind closed doors and never open coffins. No keening existed. Tears were wiped away in a hurry or choked back in shame. Death was turned into a whisper.

Just as Siobhan rose to speak at the head of the room, the lights were dimmed and candles were lit by the thin men in black suits who remained at the ready, in the wings. Guinness and whiskey were reserved for the evening hours. People would come and go all day. Laughter and stories were told. The uilleann piper would start up at dusk.

It was sometime in the middle of Siobhan's eulogy when Deirdre saw movement at the great room door. She looked over to see an older gentleman in a smart gray suit enter with an uneven gait and sit towards the back. She caught his eye, and just like the man in Ronan's photograph, she was certain this gentleman was related in some elemental way.

After she spoke, Siobhan walked to the coffin's side to pick up a small wooden container sitting next to it on the lace-covered side table. She walked towards Deirdre with confidence and a calm demeanor. The container looked like an oversized pencil box, deep and with hinges and a tarnished brass clasp. She offered it to Deirdre and told her it was hers to keep. The box had been found in the ruins of a Skibbereen building, abandoned for a century or more. The box was buried underground in a small hatch next to the hearth. On the lid was a plaque engraved: "The property of Cornelius Eoin Ó hAodha of Skibbereen."

The Man in the Gray Suit

DEIRDRE WAS AFRAID TO open the box. It looked like a miniature hope chest. She was in disbelief that it might hold a few of her great-grandfather's possessions. Was this even possible after so many years of searching through records, more and more records, ancestry documents, dead-end clues, missing birth certificates, never finding his descendants or even the parish name? Her heart skipped beats. She wondered what she might find if she reached inside. If only a trace, then she would know.

She looked up at Siobhan with a frightened expression.

"How could this be?" she managed in a breathless whisper.

Siobhan settled Deirdre's fears with a kind and knowing look and then let the keening women and wake-goers know that the reading would commence shortly.

Along with a few personal items, Siobhan had found a letter folded and tucked inside the box on top of a small leather diary. The story of Cornelius had been revealed at last. His words would put Deirdre's heart at ease. Mysteries would unravel through his own words and voice.

Just as Siobhan began reading the letter, the gray-suited gentleman at the back of the room stood up and said he would be most honored to recite the letter himself. A Corkman's voice with its strong timbre and local intonations would rouse the wake-goers, conjuring the writer's authenticity. With a twinkle in his eye, he made it known to Siobhan that he was the man for the reading. After all, he was familiar with wakes, having attended all such gatherings for the dead held in the vicinity of Abbeystrowry.

The room was silent except for a solitary house wren singing in periodic bouts of high intensity, bubbling with abrupt chirps and scolds outside the gabled window behind the coffin. No one recognized the man in the gray suit. He walked up to the coffin, laying both hands on the chest of the corpse, and began with an invocation in verse:

> *Old man from Skibbereen, how sleep comes slowly*
> *a century vanished between fields and the Celtic Sea*
> *your ghost and bones now back on Irish soil*
> *tribal blood, earthly wounds, words written*
> *with Ogham notches on mortuary stones*
> *wings ablaze from the augury's fire*
> *blessed be old man, you are home at last.*[35]

Then he quoted the book of Job 29:18:

> *In my own nest I shall grow old;*
> *I shall multiply years like the phoenix*[36]

He opened the letter, and recited every word in a familiar voice, not once looking down at the pages.

This Is My Story—The Wake of Cornelius

"My lovelies, I'm sure you'd not be thinking I'd be writing from the grave, no. But I see you gathered here today to wake the dead, to be sure. Bless you my dears for your kindness, a tad peaked from the journey, to be sure, and the long wait for me to appear out of the shadows, not knowing if I left in time, end of Dark '47 on the boat of James H. Swanton, Esq., a decent gentleman and miller of Skibbereen. Better than the coffin ships out of Queenstown. Indeed, I emigrated to England, along with one hundred famished souls sailing that day to St. David's Wales, huddled together as human ballast in the cargo pit but better than the famine pits and only a day and night crossing the ocean to Wales, however angry the sea's rollers and the listing ship's hull. You'd have it wrong if you thought I'd buy the soup and remain faithless amongst the dying and the dead. No, we were not soupers. Many perished on the roadworks or in the streets and often worse, on the fever wards of the Skibbereen Workhouse, three to a pallet and no mercy or tattered blankets to share.

"Sweet Mary Ann at my side on the gale-swept journey across the Celtic Sea, she was a true love from childhood in the village of my parents over in Lisheen Townland. Father Evin Cotter from Ballydehob took the ceremony and married us in a field behind the church, only because we couldn't manage a proper wedding, with only my brother Ryan as our witness. At the mouth of the two river fords, Ballydehob was an easy half-day's walk to Skibbereen where

I labored as a tinsmith and could scrape by with a few shillings in exchange for a dozen made pans. A tinsmith by trade. Call me a whitesmith, tinner, tinker, tinman, tinplate worker, crafting with my hand snips and shears, hammer and anvil. My best creations were my amulets of my own design. Not by chance did I become the best tin whistler in West Cork, making a few shillings at the sessions down at Annie May's Bar in Bridge Street some years before the potato turned black with misery and stink.

"Off the boat at Wales, through rough fields and valleys, then overland to London's Southwark where my tinker's talent gave us a temporary roof, whistling at night in pubs for rent or mash or both. Miraculous God, we made it, I said to Mary Ann many times over.

"Brother Ryan went up to County Galway with little brothers Liam and Darragh, identical twins and not much older than ten years. After mammy and pappy died of the relapsing fever, Ryan kept the boys under his charge. They took up beachcombing to survive, hunting seaweed for the farmers, eating dillisk and raw limpets to barely stay alive. Last I knew they went on to Inis Mór in a currach with the work boys building the stone walls all day for bread or fish. The islanders fared better during *An Gorta Mór* than in West Cork. Living off the sea for generations gave them tough *stéig*. They were accustomed to taking in food from the shores. They had the constitution to stomach sea creatures and kelp. Many in the western counties were too poor to buy even the salt needed to preserve the fish. So often the frail currach was not seaworthy in those frightful and severe winters of the early famine years, '46 and '47, bringing the dirtiest of weather. Little children searched in the woods for food, for watercress, for mushrooms, and in the bogs and mountains for berries. Along the coast, they ate seabirds and their eggs. Shellfish, sand eels, periwinkles, limpets, all varieties of seaweed were devoured, often with fatal results. There were huge pits of shells found in caves along the coast next to the skeletons of victims, dying from the uncooked and poisonous sea life ingested in desperation and hunger.

"Then there was the precarious bloodletting. Cattle and other beasts were bled at regular intervals, taken to the *log na fola*, 'the hollow of the blood,' where the choice of a skilled bloodletter was critical lest the animal weaken and perish. The blood, being the very essence of the animal's flesh, was added to various mixtures like mushrooms and cabbage, making relish cakes and baked until dry. Only cottiers lucky enough to know a kind farmer and his cow, rare indeed, would receive a ration of blood for those fortified patties.

"The ocean disentangles the netted mind, so said the ancient ones. On Inis Mór, Ryan and the boys no longer feared that the caravans and cottages in Cork would be tumbled and scorched by soulless landlords. On the island they lived for the time being in scalpeens which were better than the two-foot square allotments in the Skibbereen Workhouse.

"Sister Maeve died in the streets, piled onto the dead-cart and taken to Abbeystrowry. How many family siblings ended up in the coffinless famine pits? Did any of them make it out like Tommy Guerin? Lifted from the burial pit by the *tochaltóir uaighe*, the nameless gravediggers who crippled Tommy's knees while covering him with thin earth, striking his tiny legs with their heavy shovels. The boy lived on to tell the tale to the ripe age of sixty-five.

"The workhouses were hell on earth, as was said in hushed words around the towns and countryside. Not in your life, they declared, avoiding internment at the workhouse until near death. The sturdy stone structures, dull gray in color, were built like fortresses or prisons and meant to house sturdy beggars fit for work, as well as 'disorderly women,' foundling children, and to punish vagabonds, so the union representatives wrote in their poor laws. Only worse was Spike Island where my eldest brother Cormac, God rest his soul, was sent after he was caught stealing a meager scrap off a stale loaf from the neighbor's pantry. May he rest in peace and surely be lifted in spirit by the light in Little Nellie's window, now illuminating the fields of that island prison. Such unspeakable tortures within those walls. May Nellie's light be carrying them all now.

*

"I'll walk you back to life in Southwark now with Mary Ann well along with child. We were welcomed into the parish by the priest at St. George's where the nuns ministered to the poor and laboring mothers. If a boy, we would name him Micheál, and if a girl she would be Máire. The day finally came but ended in tragedy, God rest their souls. Mary Ann and baby Micheál died in childbirth. My heart was broken, mind stolen and locked up by grief's thieves. I became ill with melancholia and spent three months in the parish infirmary, a bleak time that was ceaseless and cast a long shadow of gray gloom over everything I saw. Was it possible to become so utterly colorblind? Indeed, grief has no bounds or laws or remedy, and our senses are cauterized by the piercing loss.

"I won't tell you the mindless work expected of the inmates while sitting about infirm, paying for care by binding sisal and ships knots and then at night counting ewes for every hour's sleeplessness. Idle and bereft, that I was.

*

"There must be a lifeline that gets tossed when matters of the heart take a toll and the lifeboat takes on water. Indeed, there was such a day. I was free at last from the infirmary where I stayed for months. The dreary winter skies were grayer than gunmetal. By Easter that spring, I was employed again by a tinplate merchant and found lodgings in the square next to St. George's with many thanks to Father Matthew, once an oblate brother in training with the Society of St. Francis.

"I began to sketch out my life's story, such as it was, mapping a treatise in verse to declare allegiance to Ireland's Brotherhood— all the nationalists that would be fighting for sovereignty and the Republic of Ireland in years to come. Curse the penal laws, stealing our language on threat of punishment with the tally sticks if we spoke so much as a word of *Gaeilge* in the classroom. Famine, pestilence, the sword, the crowbar brigades, taking it all. Riddled in misery, a burning labyrinth it was, the whole countryside a prison for the Irish people.

"And who brought the cursed blight anyway? Shipped over from the new world. The diseased potato was not born on Irish soil, I can tell you that much. Unloaded from foreign ships, spores easily spread by the wind, happy to hide in damp soil, the fungus lived all winter and spread at a ferocious speed. The blackened potatoes, full of foul-smelling disease, blacker than black, sulfurous in odor more putrid than an outhouse, rotting, caused sickness and agony when eaten. In desperation, the cottiers and their families ate those blackened potatoes. 'Food or Blood' declared the placards in the streets, the Brotherhood shouted. 'The sword of famine is less sparing than the bayonet of the soldier,'[37] wrote Thomas F. Meagher, Irish freedom fighter, hero of Waterford and leader of the Young Irelanders.

*

"I'm back in Southwark now, some years later. It was a time when I found myself lonely, wishing for the fine company of a lady again, and so I saw Miss Annie Brodie on the bridge near Southwark's market district, selling her father's produce from his country garden plot. This was a love she held for family and as the eldest girl, she took her responsibilities to heart. She was only nineteen, a bright light and young lass, a beauty who must have had more than a drop of rebel Irish blood to fall for the likes of me. I sang her a song there on the market promenade and played my best tin whistle, 'Red Is the Rose':

> Come over the hills, my bonny Irish lass
> Come over the hills to your darling
> You choose the road, love, and I'll make the vow
> And I'll be your true love forever[38]

"With her father's approval and blessings, we married that summer, his market garden in Richmond decorated for our wedding party. Annie had a green thumb as skilled as her father and so we worked and lived together at the Brodie family home. Soon the babies arrived; the first born was Liam Séamas, then Máire Eileen, followed by the youngest, Cornelius Alfred.

"The Irish Republican Brotherhood had formed the secret Fenian societies in Soho and Finsbury that year. My treatise for an independent Ireland was published in their weekly pamphlet and I was invited into the fold, much to my father-in-law Mr. Brodie's disapproval. This would only end in misery, he declared.

"Indeed, the following month while walking with my young lad Cornelius Alfred through the Southwark market, a scuffle broke out and a group of thugs came after me, pointing and shouting— 'There he is, the slum Fenian from Cork'—going for my knees, smashing them both with fury and clubs. I fell to the ground and my boy fell beside me, traumatized and sobbing. The thugs got away of course, and I was taken into care once again at St. George's infirmary, this time without much hope for healing or a cure. I was crippled badly and unable to manage work or family life. Young Cornelius Alfred was not harmed in body but was haunted for life. This was to be the beginning of the end of me I feared, as did Annie who was now left to manage the children entirely herself. I fell into a second melancholia, this time not able to shake it.

"I asked Mr. Brodie to sponsor my passage back to Cork. My homeland was where I must die, I told him, and where I'm to be buried. He did this without haste, knowing my fate was now sealed with little time left for the journey. Soon I was traveling back by merchant ship to Queenstown and then on to Skibbereen where Mr. Swanton, kind gentleman that he was, once again came to my need. He gave me a bed and meals. Not much else remains in my memory. I suppose I lingered, even occasionally played tin whistle for his children before the infection took hold and sepsis set in from my shattered knees and wounded legs. He knew to bring me to Abbeystrowry for burial when the time came.

"This is my story. God bless you all for listening."

The Stones of Abbeystrowry

THE ROOM FELL SILENT, a most unnatural circumstance at a wake. Sitting-room guests spilled out into the hallways and were now clutching glasses of Guinness and *poitín*. The man in the smart gray suit had slipped to the back of the room quite easily after his recitation of the letter. In no time he was gone altogether, without a trace, leaving the letter behind. Deirdre checked in on Éamon who was shuffling and looking weary in an uncomfortable chair. She asked if he would like refreshments with ham and tomato sandwiches that were still piled on plates in the dining room. There was more to eat than a kingly wedding buffet she thought, glancing at the sideboard and dining table, but appetites had fallen away, and the mood of the room was solemn.

Siobhan stood up at the lectern and spoke in her calm intimate voice, letting everyone know that the musicians were about to begin an open session, the perfect counterpoint for the wake ceremony and readings.

"Thanks be for the goodness of God," Éamon groaned, just like they always repeated at school after a boring class, tugging at Deirdre's sleeve and opening his fiddle case. He would sit in on the session, finally back in his element.

"What was all that about?" he asked Deirdre as he gobbled several sandwiches and slurped his tea, wondering if she knew the man in the gray suit. Éamon had attended boring old funerals at home, and this wasn't much different, he thought.

"A sad and mournful letter spoken by a heart that knew his story well." Deirdre's voice trailed off.

"Where did that old man go? He disappeared and didn't even introduce himself," Éamon complained, but his words were a jumble of noise between gobbled biscuits and sweets.

"He's likely gone to Abbeystrowry to read the stones," Deirdre said knowingly, feeling the pull herself to visit the graveyard before returning to Annie May's that evening. She knew without saying that he was the gentleman they met at the Drombeg Circle.

"Aren't you going to open the box, Miss Dee? I want to see the treasures."

"No, I'm going to wait until we are on our way back home, over the Atlantic. I've heard and seen more than I can contemplate in one day, let alone week. I'm sure there will be more surprises." In her heart, she knew it was Cornelius speaking, that there would be more to unravel before their silver bird in the sky touched down at Montreal's airport, less than three days away.

There were four musicians sitting to the right of the coffin, tuning up and looking eager to play. Some were sitting on barstools brought in for the occasion. Éamon played without missing a single beat. Many of the ornamentations he had practiced so hard for his recital were now at his fingertips. He could play as wildly as he pleased: rolls, cuts, slides, not to mention taps, *casadhs*, and *crans*. He would impress the guests as well as the keening women. Perhaps they would wail along to the songs.

Even though the wake would carry on well into the early hours of the next day, Deirdre knew it was time for them to leave, especially if they wanted the last of the twilight to visit the graveyard. Siobhan arranged for one of the ancestry guests to take them back to their inn.

The visit to Abbeystrowry cemetery was a quiet reprieve after the crowded proceedings at the wake.

Everywhere the stones were calling, calling to her for recognition and peace.

"*Suaimhneas Síoraí Air, Go Raibh Suaimhneas Síoraí Air*—
Eternal Rest Be Upon Him"—one after another. This one captured
her attention:

*Eternal rest grant unto them, O Lord, and let perpetual light
shine upon them. Like the seed buried in the ground, you have produced the harvest of eternal life for us.*

Deirdre stopped at the memorial monument, erected in 1887
by Eugene McCarthy, a blacksmith of Ilen Street in Skibbereen.
This was the spot where an entire generation of Skibbereen people
lay buried, all in the space of a year and a half. The monster graves,
often referred to as the famine pits, held the coffinless dead who
were piled by the hundreds, without mourning, without family,
and most certainly dumped in the dead of night.

"*Go ndēana Dia trōcaire ar an-anamacha*—May God
have mercy on many souls"—the words spoken in her dream at
Glendalough.

Deirdre's driver from the ancestry group, a young man
named Daniel, was restless to get on their way back to Skibbereen.
Twilight had nearly vanished; there was only a trace of the waning
moonlight, mostly hidden behind clouds. Just as she walked back
towards Éamon and Daniel, she heard something rustling in the
leaves of the hawthorn bush to the right of the cemetery gate. She
thought she saw a shape, the outline of a hat, just shy of her eye's
focus. She also detected the sweet aroma of pipe tobacco. She bent
down to lay a small stone—a black tourmaline—in remembrance
of her ancestors. She had carried the crystal in her special whiskey
pouch for longer than she could remember. Deirdre knew this was
the place where it belonged.

> *I will whisper*
> *secrets in your ear,*
> *Just nod yes*
> *and be silent.*[39]

PART FOUR

A Lamp, a Lifeboat, a Ladder

Be a lamp or a lifeboat or a ladder. Help someone's soul heal.
Walk out of your house like a Shepherd.[40]

—RUMI

Tramore Strand and Back to Dublin

THE SUN WAS UP and shining through the thin lace curtains in Annie May's second-story windows long before Deirdre and Éamon woke up. They went downstairs to the dining tables for a full Irish breakfast before packing up for the day of travel back to Dublin. It was under six hours if the roads were clear. There would be plenty of time to stop for an early afternoon break from the drive. They were both tired from the intense days spent in Skibbereen, attending the players' readings that first night followed by a long day's wake, not to mention a most unexpected eulogy and reading by the stranger in the gray suit. This must have been what Siobhan meant when she said there would be surprises for Deirdre when she arrived in Skibbereen, and mysteries solved regarding her family. There was no doubt the gentleman at the wake was an incarnation of her great-grandfather, if not his very ghost. How could he recite the entire letter so passionately otherwise? It felt like he was speaking to her directly, often catching her gaze as he paused his words. His natural manner and authentic expressions of sorrow made his storytelling feel deeply personal. Emotion welled up in his eyes frequently. It was a mournful and familiar story for the wake-goers, the families of victims, and survivors of *An Gorta Mor.*

Deirdre and Éamon set off before nine, planning their route through Waterford where they would take a walk along Tramore Beach, a golden sandy strand stretching three miles with dunes, known as the Rabbit Burrows at the far end of the beach. This would be their chance to breathe the wild open air from the Celtic

Sea and maybe even take a dip into those aqua green waves. The drive was under three hours. The beach would make a good rest stop before they carried on to Dublin, another two hours away.

The road travel gave Deirdre and Éamon time to share their thoughts and experiences; reflections on St. Kevin's Cell and the Round Tower, the unworldly faith of Little Nellie, Éamon's recital and the tune of the faeries from the Blasket Islands, their journey to Drombeg Circle and Skibbereen . . . They both held on to different memories and spoke of their journey's challenges. The wake was especially difficult for Éamon. He was aware of *An Gorta Mór* from lessons in his Celtic music classes at St. Anne's. He knew about famine commemorations which now take place internationally, but it was hard for him to comprehend the political implications which are controversial subjects even to this day. The Heritage Center now attracts thousands of visitors every year. Many take part in the Skibbereen Famine Trail, a walking tour that includes the solemn sites linked to the Great Hunger. Over two million people left Ireland during *An Gorta Mór*, and the Irish diaspora includes over one hundred million worldwide.

"How could so many be left to die of hunger and disease when there was plenty of food sent by ship out of the country the whole time?" Éamon asked, not able to grasp cruelty and neglect of that magnitude. Mahoney's descriptions and sketches left haunting images in his mind, especially the story of Tommy Guerin and how he was left for dead in a shallow grave.

Deirdre had no answers for Éamon. She was helpless herself to shake off the images and wondered how much ancestral memory she carried. Often her emotions ran away with her at the most inopportune times. Her great-grandfather's many losses and melancholia, which he so vividly described in his letter, echoed in her bones. Now she knew why the well of tears would not run dry.

When they reached the Tramore Strand they were revitalized by the cool salty sea air. The water was a vivid aquamarine with frothy white waves slapping the shoreline. It was easy to wade far out in the shallows, so they rolled up pant legs and ran out, feeling the weight of their journey wash away on each wave. They picked a few rayed trough shells, white and shiny, wet in the sun. Deirdre would add them to her pouch of gems and stones.

"Éamon, I am certain you will be back on scholarship one day. Your recital was masterly. The room was dead silent when you played. I heard the woman next to me inhale a long sharp breath as you began the haunting Blasket piece. How perfect it was that they chose the very music you had prepared so exquisitely at home."

"I guess we will call in to the music director when we get back to Sandymount in Dublin," Éamon suggested, sounding excited again.

"We will, and I'd bet you ten Irish punts that you've won the scholarship!"

*

It was going on five o'clock when they arrived at Sandymount lodgings in Dublin. The concierge seemed to know them right away and handed them keys and several envelopes, one being a special delivery from Cork College. Éamon tore open the letter on the spot. The words were printed in bold:

"Éamon Patrick O'Connor, you have been awarded a full scholarship to attend undergraduate studies at University Cork College Music Department, *Roinn an Cheoil*. We welcome you and applaud your brilliance and unique musical talent. Your Irish heritage most certainly shines through you. Your music studies here in Cork will make your family proud."

They sat for a long while in the lobby, stunned and excited, unable to speak. Even though Deirdre was certain he would win the scholarship, she felt a rush of adrenaline and pride for Éamon's gifts and determination. She also knew he was born with Irish blood and music most certainly ran through his veins.

"Miss Dee, open the other letter, it is addressed to you from Kinsale."

Deirdre had forgotten there was another envelope. She tore it open but was quiet for a moment, not wanting to reveal the words right away. It was from Rory. He was inviting her to teach at the

115

children's summer music school in Kinsale for two weeks at the beginning of August.

"Come back," he wrote. "We need you here. You will shine brighter than any of the other teachers. The music society will pay your way. Please come."

*

It was a fitful night with little sleep for Deirdre at Sandymount. A quick supper at Whitty's and then preparations for their flight the next morning from Dublin was all they managed. It would be a long haul of a travel day, including the flight change at Heathrow. They would land on the same day in Montreal by midafternoon.

"Good night. *Oíche Mhaith*," they both said, practicing their Irish.

PART FIVE

Up and Away

Beannacht ar an mhuintir síorraí!
Blessings for the Eternal Family

The Diary of Cornelius

THE SILVER BIRD WITH the shamrock tail took them back across the Irish Sea and then the British Airways jumbo bird set off, Montreal-bound. June was a good month to fly. The skies were clear. They were going towards the light, not losing time, as if captured in the stratosphere by a dream, not traveling but floating over the Atlantic.

Once they could no longer see the land mass below, just water, Éamon pressed Deirdre to open the treasure box that Siobhan had given her at the wake. Deirdre had packed it safely into her carry-on bag.

The wooden box had a distinct scent, a mix of earth and clay and tobacco, and kind of musty too. It was rectangular, at least a foot long and plenty deep. They were both nervous, apprehensive about what they might discover inside.

The brass hinges were stiff and creaked as Deirdre opened the lid. On the top was the handwritten letter presented at the wake, tucked on top of a small leather book, most likely a diary. Underneath was a clay pipe and a small tin whistle, marked with the inscription "*Hi-D.*" At the bottom of the box was a very tarnished copper pendant, barely showing its full design under a patina of greenish blue, caked from a century of oxidation. Deirdre rubbed the pendant until she could see its design underneath—the Ogham stone—identical to her own missing pendant, but in copper and not silver. She knew about copper jewelry from the shop in Toronto's Yorkville where she had often looked for old amulets and earrings and learned how copper is alloyed by mixing one part tin with nine parts copper granules. The crucible is lined with flux to remove impurities from the molten metal. She was attracted to copper for its healing properties, for wound healing and bone strength.

"Will you wear the pendant, Miss Dee?" Éamon asked, holding it up near her neck. She switched out her necklace and chain she was wearing. The pendant fit perfectly. Even with the heavy patina it was beautiful. She liked its old appearance. Deirdre could smell the scent of pipe mingling with copper. Cornelius's craftsmanship no doubt.

"What about the diary, Miss Dee?"

She was scared to open it in case the pages fell apart but was surprised that it remained intact and mostly legible, even with the brittle, yellowing paper. The handwriting was elegant, written with a blue fountain pen. Deirdre flipped through the pages knowing the diary would provide her with many more clues about Cornelius and her Irish family. She looked at the closing pages, noticing the larger print, written like a dedication or announcement. This is what it said:

> Deirdre Máire Ó hAodha, granddaughter of Liam Séamas, my own great-granddaughter, may you live a long life and always play fiddle with me.
>
> Éamon Patrick O'Connor, great-grandson of Cornelius Ailbhe, my own great-great-grandson, may you live a long life in Ireland and play fiddle to your heart's content.

Éamon was dumfounded, his cheeks flushed while his intense eyes searched for reassurance as Deirdre read the diary entry. She smiled with soft eyes. Her great-grandfather's gift of second sight had blessed her for many years. This was his gift to her.

"Would you have guessed, Miss Dee?"

"I knew without knowing," she answered.

At the back of the diary, on the inside cover, was written: *A Lamp, A Lifeboat, A Ladder.*

Éamon looked over to Deirdre just as the server came by with drinks. She ordered a pint of Guinness, and he ordered one too. Up and away in the silver bird, he was allowed whatever he wished, even a pint.

"We are cousins, Miss Dee!" He was enthralled by the diary's revelation. They were family now. He took a hearty sip of Guinness.

"Yes indeed," Deirdre said with joy in her expression, knowing that Éamon's musical mastery of the fiddle must be in his Ó hAodha blood, *this cartography of genes.*

Sláinte. Beannacht ar an mhuintir síorraí! Blessings for the eternal family.

Endnotes

1. Hayes, "Notations on a Map," 60–65.
2. Hayes, "To the Shores of Port Phillip Bay."
3. Traditional Irish Song, "Siúil a Rúin."
4. Traditional Irish Lullaby, "Too-ra-loo-ra-loo-ral."
5. Irish Folk Song, "Dear Old Skibbereen."
6. Joyce, *Finnegan's Wake*, 208, 412.
7. Scottish Traditional Song, "The Parting Glass."
8. Traditional Irish Blessing, "St. Brigid's Blessing."
9. Irish Folk Song, "Dear Old Skibbereen."
10. Hayes, "Silver Mistress of Our Dreams," 83–84.
11. Hayes, "Notations on a Map," 60–65.
12. Whyte, "Well of Grief," 95.
13. Synge, *Deirdre of the Sorrows*, 211–268
14. Whyte, "Well of Grief," 95.
15. Haggerty, "St. Kevin, Founder of Glendalough."
16. Hayes, "Wishing Cross at Gleann Dá Loch." 78.
17. Haggerty, "St. Kevin—Founder of Glendalough."
18. Heaney, "St. Kevin and the Blackbird," 9–10.
19. Heaney, "St. Kevin and the Blackbird," 9–10.
20. Heaney, "St. Kevin and the Blackbird," 9–10.
21. Traditional Irish Song, "*Oró, Sé Do Bheatha 'Bhaile*."
22. Tagore, "Faith Is the Bird."
23. Matthew 19:14

24. Boyd, *Daily Afflictions*, 89.

25. Wilcox, "Worth While," 10.

26. O'Donovan Rossa, "Voice from Ireland," 91.

27. O'Donovan Rossa, "Song of Freedom," 23.

28. Hayes, "Notations on a Map," 60–65.

29. Hayes, "Notations on a Map," 60–65.

30. Irish Folk Song, "Dear Old Skibbereen."

31. Kearney and O'Regan, *Skibbereen: The Famine Story*.

32. Daly, "Heir Island," 38–40.

33. St. John, "The Fields of Atherny."

34. Hawkes, *Cell-Level Healing*, 56.

35. Hayes, "How Sleep Comes Slowly." Unpublished poem.

36. Job 29:18.

37. Meagher, *Meagher of the Sword*, 56.

38. Traditional Irish Ballad, "Red Is the Rose."

39. Rumi, "I will whisper / secrets in your ear. / Just nod yes / and be silent."

40. Rumi, "Be a Lamp, a Lifeboat, a Ladder."

Glossary of Irish Words and Phrases

Annwn: The Otherworld

a *tórramh*: a wake, or a *faire*, a communal wake

An Gorta Mór: The Great Hunger

An Tíogar Ceilteach: Celtic Tiger (Ireland's Economic Miracle)

Casadhs: turns [in music]

Ceridwen and *Taliesin*: Celtic goddess and god of music

Chucky (Poblachtach): Irish Republican

Cloch-Cheacal Agus Cairn: Drombeg Circle, meaning "the small ridge"

Cloigtheach: bell tower

Cóemgen: St. Kevin, translates to "beautiful shining birth"

Crann sailí: the willow tree

Crans: a musical ornamentation where a note is played and repeated two or three times with a cut just before it

Fáinleog: Barn Swallows

Fulacht Fiadh: a well-preserved prehistoric mound of heat-altered stone

Gaeilge: Irish language

Gaeltacht: the regions in Ireland in which the Irish language is, or was until recently, the primary spoken language

Gealbhan Binne: Little House Sparrow

Gleann Dá Loch: Valley of the Lakes

Gleann Scáth an Bháis: Valley of the Shadow of Death

Go ndēana Dia trōcaire ar an-anamacha: "May God have mercy on many souls"

log na fola: "the hollow of the blood" where bloodletting of livestock took place

mná chaointe: keening woman

Ogham: named after *Oghma*, the Celtic god of elocution or fine speech

Oíche Mhaith: good night

Oró, Sé Do Bheatha 'Bhaile: "Oh, It's Your Home Life"

Poitín: anglicized as "poteen," a traditional Irish distilled beverage, initially made from malted barley, but later from other fermentable crops including sugar beet and potatoes

Port na bPúcaí: song of the spirits, or tune of the fairies

Roinn an Cheoill: Music Department

Ruairí: boy's name Rory

Sceach Gheal: Sacred Hawthorn

Sé an Tiarna m'Aoire: The Lord is My Shepherd

Siúil: walk

Sláinte. Beannacht ar an mhuintir síorraí: Blessings for the eternal family

spioraid na sinsear: ancestral spirit caught between this world and the next

Suaimhneas Síoraí Air, Go Raibh Suaimhneas Síoraí Air: Eternal Rest Be Upon Him

Thevshi: a spirit caught between this world and the next

Tine Cnáimh: fire of bones, Bonna Night

Tiocfaidh ár lá: our day will come

tochaltóir uaighe: nameless gravediggers

For pronunciation of words in Irish: https://www.focloir.ie/en/dictionary/ei/pronunciation

Irish phonology varies from dialect to dialect; there is no standard pronunciation of Irish.

Bibliography

Boyd, Andrew. *Daily Afflictions: The Agony of Being Connected to Everything in the Universe.* New York: Norton, 2002.

Daly, Eugene. *Heir Island: Its History and People.* Cork, IE: Heron's Way, 2004.

Haggerty, Bridget. "St. Kevin—Founder of Glendalough." Irish Culture and Customs, September 27, 2024. https://www.irishcultureandcustoms.com/ASaints/Kevin.html.

Hayes, Diana. "Notations on a Map, Looking for Cornelius." In *Labyrinth of Green*, 60–65. Oakville, ON: Plumleaf, 2019.

———. "The Silver Mistress of Our Dreams." In *This Is the Moon's Work: New and Selected Poems*, 83–84. Salt Spring Island, BC: Mother Tongue, 2011.

———. "The Wishing Cross at Gleann Da Loch." In *This is the Moon's Work: New and Selected Poems*, 78. Salt Spring Island, BC: Mother Tongue, 2011.

Hawkes, Joyce Whiteley. *Cell-Level Healing: The Bridge from Soul to Cell.* New York: Simon & Schuster, 2006.

Heaney, Seamus. "St. Kevin and the Blackbird." In *Field Work*, 9–10. Essex: Faber and Faber, 1979.

Joyce, James. *Finnegan's Wake.* London: Faber and Faber. 1939.

Kearney, Terri, and Philip O'Regan. *Skibbereen: The Famine Story.* West Cork, IE: Macalla, 2015.

Meagher, Thomas Francis. *Meagher of the Sword: Speeches of Thomas Francis Meagher in Ireland, 1846–1848, His Narrative of Events in Ireland in July 1848, Personal Reminiscences of Waterford, Galway, and His Schooldays.* Edited by Arthur Griffith. Dublin: M. H. Gill & Son, 1917.

O'Donovan Rossa, Mary Jane. "A Voice from Ireland." In *Irish Lyrical Poems*, 91. New York: P. M. Haverty, 1868.

———. "A Song of Freedom." In *Irish Lyrical Poems*, 23. New York: P. M. Haverty, 1868.

St. John, Pete. "The Fields of Athenry." Dublin: Estate of Pete St. John.

Synge, John Millington. *Deirdre of the Sorrows.* In *The Complete Plays*, 211–68. New York: Vintage, 1935.

Tragore, Rabindranth. "Faith Is the Bird." In *Fireflies*, 185. Hubbardston, MA: Asphodel, 2014.

Whyte, David. "The Well of Grief." In *River Flow: New and Selected Poems*, 95. Langley, WA: Many Rivers, 2007.

Wilcox, Ella Wheeler. "Worth While." In *Poems of Cheer*, 10. London: Gay & Hancock, 1908.

www.ingramcontent.com/pod-product-compliance
Lightning Source LLC
Chambersburg PA
CBHW060423260626
47161CB00005B/1762